THE ABSOLUTELY TRUE STORY OF US

Melanie Marchande

ISBN-13: 978-1507641378
ISBN-10: 1507641370

D1527150

Table of Contents

Chapter One - M

1

Chapter Two - Based on a True Story

13

Chapter Three - Master

23

Chapter Four - The Wager

32

Chapter Five - A Decent Proposal

44

Chapter Six - The Gang's All Here

54

Chapter Seven - Leather and Laces

63

Chapter Eight - For You

75

Chapter Nine - The Storm

86

Chapter Ten - What Happened

102

Chapter Eleven - Darts

113

Chapter Twelve - A Hill of Beans

120

Chapter Thirteen - Third Time's the Charm

129

Chapter Fourteen - The Park

140

Chapter Fifteen - Meeting M

147

Chapter Sixteen - Wanted

162

CHAPTER ONE

M

There are only two people in the world that I truly hate. One of them is unpacking his toothbrush in my bathroom, and the other one is texting me to find out what color my panties are.

How do I get myself into these situations?

Oh, right. Because I'm a liar.

Don't judge me too fast - you know you do it too. Most lies are harmless. I thought mine was, too. But I'm starting to wonder.

My phone buzzes.

Come on babe. Don't keep me waiting, you know how I feel about that.

With a sigh, I tap out a quick response. I don't even remember what underwear I've got on, and I'm certainly not going to check. My ex-boyfriend is ten feet away, arranging his toiletries. In *my* bathroom.

Black lace

I send the message quickly and shove my phone back into my pocket. "Don't get too comfortable in there," I call out to my ex, hurrying over to make sure he's not messing with my stuff.

"Not much risk of that," he says. "With you breathing down my neck as usual."

So, why is my ex moving back in with me? Has he fallen on hard times? Am I that much of a bleeding heart?

No. Well. Not anymore.

He's actually helping *me* out, but you wouldn't know it.

My phone buzzes again, and I resolutely ignore it. But for a "silent" setting, it's pretty damn far from silent. Dean, my ex, glances at me.

"You're blowing up tonight," he comments. The unspoken part is *who on earth would be texting* you?

"Yeah, it turns out there are some guys who actually answer their messages." I cross my arms, leaning against the doorway. "I hope you brought your own toothpaste. I don't want you rubbing whatever skank-germs you've got in your mouth all over my Crest."

"Oh, so there's a *guy* involved." He shoots me that lopsided grin in the mirror, and I draw my lips a little tighter together. "Just one?"

The jig is up, more or less. I pull my phone out of

my pocket and glance over the message, keeping a straight face as best I can, even as a hot blush starts to creep up the back of my neck.

"I didn't say that," I point out. "But yeah, I'm not one to juggle. I know that's hard for you to wrap your head around, but..."

"Right." He chuckles. "I'm the man-whore. Remind me what other sins I've supposedly committed? Sometimes it's hard to keep track."

I stalk into the next room without another word. That's the most infuriating thing about him - after all this time, after all the damning evidence, he still refuses to admit it.

Fumbling my phone back out of my pocket, I glare at the message. Oh, how I wish it didn't make my throat tighten.

You don't even know what this guy looks like.

Yeah, well I know what parts of him look like.

Don't be alarmed. I'm an author; we talk to ourselves all the time. It's totally normal.

Probably.

I just keep staring at the screen, until the words stop making any kind of sense, until it actually seems like starting this virtual affair was a good idea.

Lace. Perfect. I love the ripping sound it makes between my teeth.

My mystery man has a bit of an oral fixation. At first, I just played along, because I never really understood the appeal. Back in the day, Dean gave it the good ol' college try, but whatever near-spiritual experience most women seem to have under a guy's tongue - it's just not there for me. I don't know, maybe I'm defective. But damned if the way Mystery Man describes it doesn't get my heart racing.

He talks about the way he wants to devour me, slow and then fast and then slow again, how I'll coat his chin with my juices, and all that good stuff. There's something about the words he uses. It's like I can almost *feel* it.

I really hate how much the Mystery Man affects me, almost as much as I hate the man himself. It's just not right. If he's getting off on this, I'm sure it's only because of the power he has over me. It wasn't enough for him to just crush my books, he's got to crush me, too. I'm sure that's what this is leading up to. He wants to string me along and then watch me fall.

Okay, let's back up. Let me try to explain.

Mystery Man is, well, a mystery. Nobody knows his true identity, or if he's even really a he. I have strong reasons to suspect that he is, although I suppose those pictures could've been stolen off of Craigslist or something. But I did a reverse image search on everything he sent me; I'm not stupid. As far as I can tell, he's genuine.

He's also a book reviewer. He calls himself M. As much as I don't want to give him the credit, it's a lot easier to just say M rather than Mystery Man, so let's just make a graceful transition.

I have to admit, M's gimmick is a rather good one. He says he's providing the male point of view on romance novels, and often focuses his rant-reviews on the behavior of the male love interests and how realistic, or not, their behavior is.

The thing is, M is funny. M is *really* funny. I understand why people gobble up his reviews with a spoon, especially because he doesn't treat authors with kid gloves. Before I hit it big, I used to love snickering over his blog. It's always fun to throw stones, until one day you wake up and *you're* the target.

It's his internet-given right to hate my books, and I'd never dream of taking that away from him. But he seems to glory in it. I don't think it's just my natural bias; his review of my last book was absolutely vicious, and oddly personal. When I first saw it, I pretty much laughed it off. I mean, the guy doesn't know me. Imagine the nerve of him, painting me as some impossible harpy based solely on my book. Writing me off as a sexually frustrated, possibly frigid woman just waiting for Prince Charming to come along...I mean, he's not necessarily wrong about the sexually frustrated part, but the rest? Hell. I'm not waiting for Prince Charming. Not anymore. I'd settle for Prince Tolerable.

I make it a policy not to respond to reviews. They're for other readers, not for me. I read them, I learn from them, but I know it's weird and invasive to join a conversation that I'm not meant to be a part of. But M was begging me - literally - to explain myself. I understood it was probably rhetorical, but it was so tempting.

Still. I didn't take the bait.

At first.

He started needling me on Twitter. Poking and prodding, and I was determined to ignore him, until one night I had a few too many glasses of wine and made the second biggest mistake of my life.

We'll get to Mistake Number One in a minute.

I actually responded to M. Privately. I knew there was a chance it would end up on his blog anyway, so I was nice enough about it - just told him he could't expect me to engage with him. I wasn't that kind of author. If he wanted drama, he'd have to go elsewhere.

He responded privately, which surprised me.

I'm not into drama, I just have this morbid fascination with what makes you tick.

My heart, for some reason, skipped a few beats.

Okay, so maybe I had a little bit of a weird, twisted crush on this guy. Maybe I've had it for a while. I've always enjoyed a good dose of snark when it's well aimed, which is one reason why I feel like such a hypocrite for the way my stomach roils when he writes about me. But it's only natural. Anyone would feel the same way.

After a few minutes without a response, he messaged me again.

The character limit is killing me. Check your FB.

Against my better judgment, I did. It took a few minutes, but I wasn't disappointed.

M: Look doll, you know it's nothing personal, this is just my job. I can't give people special treatment. You seem like a nice person and a real professional which I appreciate. I don't make friends with authors because it's a conflict of interest, but if you want to do an interview for my blog I bet a lot of people would love to see it. Promise I won't twist your words.

An interview? With M? Yeah, right. It would be great exposure, but at what cost? I told him:

Thanks, but no thanks. Not interested in your Freudian analysis.

I don't know why that popped out. I guess the fact that he correctly pegged me as sexually frustrated was bothering me more than I realized. He replied:

M: Tell me I'm wrong, and I'll apologize.

He knew I couldn't. Gritting my teeth, I shot back:

You're just playing the odds. Most women are sexually frustrated because most men are terrible in bed. Keep gloating all you want, but the odds are not in your favor.

I felt triumphant for all of forty-five seconds before he came back with:

M: Where'd you get those statistics from, sunshine? The Institute of Sour Grapes?

Damn it. He was just as quick in real time as he was on his blog.

See, the dirty secret of most writers is we need a lot of time to seem clever. I always figured he was one of those, but he seemed to be a true wit, which was infuriating. It took me a while to come up with a response.

Don't worry, I'm sure you're very good. Or at the very

least, you THINK you are, which is all that really matters, right?

He started typing back almost immediately.

M: I know you expect me to make some kind of crude joke about proving it to you, but I'm not "that guy."

I rolled my eyes.

Sure. You don't need to be. I'm sure you get plenty of action from those desperate groupies.

To say that M has fans is an understatement. He presents himself as a moderately attractive, self-confident man in the romance world, so of course he draws attention. It's easy, like being the only guy in ballet or yoga class. He's got women hanging on to his every word, and it's only made his ego swell bigger.

He finally responded.

M: I don't screw around with fans.

My eyebrows went up.

I didn't expect you to be so principled.

His reply made me chuckle a little.

M: It's not principled. Have you ever fucked someone who worships you? It's not that fun. Hate sex is always better.

It took me a second to realize what he was

implying. Unless - no. I was almost positive. M, king of snark, was *hitting on me*.

What the hell was I going to say?

Finally, I gave up on being clever.

I wouldn't know.

Again, his response came quickly.

M: Oh. That's tragic. There's nothing quite like the turn-on of somebody who hates you, but can't control how much they want you.

I downed the rest of my glass of wine before I answered.

I guess I've never had the opportunity to find out.

Your move, M.

M: Too bad. You have a dirty mind. I bet you're fun in bed if somebody can manage to pry your chastity belt off.

My face was burning. I should've closed the window, should've walked away, but I didn't.

I'm not wearing a chastity belt.

All I could hear was my heart pounding in my ears while I waited for him to answer.

M: So what ARE you wearing?

I swallowed, hard.

You're totally failing at not being "that guy," you know.

There was slight pause before his response.

M: At this moment, I find I don't really care.

And then, I made the decision that sealed my fate.

Black pencil skirt. No panties.

There was another pause before he responded, and I didn't want to think about why. Except I did. I really, really did.

M: I don't believe you. Keep going.

So that's how it started, with me and M.

I'll never know what would've happened between us if I hadn't brought up the topic of sex in our first real exchange. Maybe nothing. Or maybe it was an inevitability. The conversation could have died out there, but it didn't. Instead, we embarked on a torrid, virtual affair that consumes way too much of my time and energy.

Back to the present day. I still haven't answered his last text, the one about wanting to rip my panties off with his teeth. The last thing I want is to go all jelly-legged with lust while my ex-boyfriend is unpacking in the next room, and I know that's the effect M has on me.

My phone buzzes again.

M: Take them off.

My breath catches in my throat. It's insane, *obscene*, that this guy can have such an effect on me. We've never even met. He has no idea what I look like, beyond a small headshot on my website.

If I'm being honest, that last bit might be my favorite part.

I can't.

M: Yes you can.

I'm not alone.

M: So excuse yourself.

How can I explain this situation to M? There's no way I'm telling him the truth. He'd tell the whole world, and everything would come crashing down.

More importantly, why do I feel like I have to? I always have the option of just telling him to fuck off, and he wouldn't be able to do a damn thing about it. But I won't.

Because with M, I'm not just Felicity Warden, frumpy failure with a big ass who only stumbled into success by telling a whopper of a lie. With M, I can be anybody.

There's a tapping at the door.

"What?" I demand, yanking it open.

"Uh." Dean clears his throat. "If your parents are

coming over here, shouldn't my stuff be in your room?"

"They're not going to be snooping," I insist.

"You want to take that risk?" he asks. "Look, I'll sleep on the sofa, obviously - but we should at least make it *look* like we're living together."

He has a point. I hate it when he has a point.

My phone buzzes again, and I want to throw it against the wall.

"Sorry," says Dean. "I don't mean to interrupt your vigorous texting schedule, but I figured I should hang up my shirts in here."

I stalk past him and lock myself in the bathroom, pulling out my phone as soon as it's safe.

M: Well?

I'm serious. I can't. I'm wearing jeans anyway.

M: Don't care. Do it. When you feel the seam of the denim pressing into your bare pussy, you'll think about me.

Somehow, in that moment, the sensible corner of my brain kicks in. However brief, it's enough for me to quickly type:

Sorry. I have to go.

I lock my phone and shove it back into my pocket, breathing hard.

How did I end up like this?

CHAPTER TWO

Based on a True Story

Six Months Ago

It all starts with five little words.

Based on a true story.

I'm at the dollar theater with my friend Jack, splitting the bag of popcorn I smuggled in, thanks to my cavernous oversized purse. I feel kind of bad. I know these places barely make any money as it is, and I'm only making things worse by refusing to buy their shrink-wrapped cookies with the pink frosting. But I haven't sold an article in ages, and Jack is just as broke as I am. He's been job-hunting for three years now. At this point, filling out applications pretty much *is* his full-time job.

Me, I'm still holding onto the great American

dream: self-employment. Owning a business. Being an entrepreneur. Working from home. Bathrobes. Fuzzy slippers. Mail order groceries. Tequila at nine A.M. I won so many writing awards in college I could wallpaper my living room with them, so why the hell can't I make my living as a writer?

That question stopped being rhetorical some time ago.

"Hey, stop being greedy." Jack tries to swat my hand out of the way, nearly overturning the bag in the process.

I squeal at him, saving it just in time. "For God's sake. You're like the dog in that fable who drops the bone in the water when he sees his reflection. *You* stop being greedy, or neither one of us gets any popcorn." He's rolling his eyes, but I decide to ignore that. "Besides, I brought it."

"*Besides, I brought it,*" Jack echoes, in an obnoxious falsetto. "That's you. That's what you sound like right now."

By all rights, I should hate Jack. I met him in a dive bar shortly after Dean left, during one of my brave attempts to "put myself out there." The sexual chemistry was nil, but we fell hard for each other as friends and have been completely inseparable since. He's a gorgeous player with a killer smile, but my libido remains stubbornly disinterested. Thankfully, the feeling's mutual - which is slightly less surprising on his side.

Well, he might be a player, but he's no Dean. He doesn't get involved with women who have romantic commitments, and he never breaks hearts on purpose. So he's got that going for him. I wouldn't be able to stand his company if he was that kind of scumbag.

"Look. *Based on a true story*." Jack points at the screen. "I can't wait until this comes out on Redbox and we can do a drinking game."

"We could've done one now," I observe. "Want me to go hit the liquor store across the street? It's not like they're searching bags here."

"It's eleven-thirty in the morning," he observes, raising his eyebrow at me. "Have some morals, Warden."

"Neither of us have jobs, *Harrison*." I laugh at him. Thankfully, we're the only ones in the theater, so we get to enjoy ourselves. "There's nothing immoral about day-drinking when you have no responsibilities."

"Yeah, but there is something immoral about me carting your drunk ass home. Never again, I swear. Didn't even get a blowjob out of it." He winks at me.

"You want one?" I flick a piece of popcorn at his lap.

"Ask me again in ten years, if we're both still single." Suddenly, he sits up straighter. "Shit, I just thought of the best plot for a romantic-comedy-porno ever."

"Oh, great, I hear that's a super lucrative genre right now." I roll my eyes at him. "Okay, so...which part of this is based on a true story?"

"That part," he says, pointing at the lead actor taking a drink. "One of the family members probably drank soda at some point, right?"

Snickering, I lean back in my seat. "Okay, but seriously. It has to be something more than that."

"No, it doesn't." He turns to look at me. "Wait, are you serious? You actually think they have to back up their claims when they say that? Nobody asks."

I guess I've never thought about it before. "So, you

can just make up any bullshit you want and claim it's true? And nobody can sue you?"

"I mean, as long as it's not about anyone in particular, sure." Jack shrugs. "Who cares? Who's gonna find out?"

The seed of an idea is germinating in my mind. I can't even focus on the movie when shit starts to go crazy, because I'm still thinking about what Jack said.

Last year, I did try my hand at writing a romance novel. It's the most lucrative genre in fiction, and I guess I wanted to prove a point to myself. I managed to get some good reviews and make enough to cover the editing costs, but it became very clear that it wasn't going to be my new career. I just didn't get it. Clearly, I didn't understand what the market wanted. I swore I'd never do it again, but now I'm starting to reconsider.

Rom-com porno *sounds* ridiculous, but in this post Fifty Shades world, I know steamy romance is hugely popular. And "based on a true story" as a hook? I could do a lot worse.

It's been a while since I tried to write fiction. Before the last novel, it had been even longer. My parents always gently discouraged me from it, saying it was impossible to make a career out of it. Unless I was lucky enough to become the next Stephen King or James Patterson, there were a lot more practical ways to spend my time.

A plot is starting to unwind itself in my mind, and not even the jump scares can shake me out of it. I can already see the movie trailer set to Carolina Liar's "Show Me What I'm Looking For." It's beautiful, sexy, inspiring. I'll hit every bestseller list, win every award.

"Psst." Jack snaps his fingers in my face. "Where'd you wander off to?"

"I got an idea," I tell him, slowly, still staring at the screen but not really seeing it. "An idea for a book."

Back at home, I nibble on the edge of my fingernail. Am I really going to do this? It's so easy: just five little words. A lie, but a harmless one. I'm not even pretending to be an addict or a trauma survivor or anything like that, and besides, people lie like this all the time. Like the people who made that movie. They don't expect me to believe some family was really terrorized by a demon that was attached to a haunted doll, do they? It's artistic license. It's an acceptable falsehood.

Nobody will ever know.

I've already got a perfectly serviceable pen name, with one sad, languishing book I never bothered to un-publish. So why not? What's stopping me?

I crack my knuckles, and then I start to type.

The book begins to form before my eyes. I call it *Mergers & Acquisitions*, because I'm being terribly clever. Boy meets girl, boy and girl are competing for the same job, claws out, sex - and eventually love - ensues. It's pretty standard stuff, but the hook gives it more depth. More character.

Fake character. But character all the same.

As I write, I let pieces of my personality seep into the main character-slash-author. I am Lana DeVane, and Lana is me. The hero, Damien, is everything I know the reading public wants. Dominant, demanding, arrogant.

Sexy and loyal as hell. Smart and sarcastic and successful. By the end, I'm practically in love with him. Too bad guys like that don't seem to exist. Particularly the "loyal" part.

Anyway, readers love it. Just as I thought, they love him even more than I do. Sometimes my predictions actually come true.

Of course, I didn't predict that within two months of publishing the book, I'd have the opportunity to be interviewed for an online news segment about successful romance author-entrepreneurs. One I couldn't pass up. I don't use my real name, but I have no choice but to use my real face.

And they want to meet the guy.

Well, it's only natural.

Jack is the first person I ask, of course. He laughs in my face and tells me he's not getting mixed up in my drama. Sometimes that guy is just too damn smart.

That only leaves one option, really.

Dean.

Ugh.

We're still on civil terms, more or less, in spite of everything. And he'll probably feel obligated enough to say yes. We've got a history. We can fake the chemistry easily enough.

Harmless, right?

Of course, I also don't predict that one of my sisters will stumble across the video and discover my secret identity. And that my whole family is going to read the damn book and completely lose their minds, wanting to get to know this amazing, romantic specimen of a man.

They've met Dean at a few holiday get-togethers, but they always seemed to have trouble remembering his name. As a middle child among six siblings, it's easy to overlook me. And I've never really minded it - at least, that's what I tell myself.

The interview was a cakewalk. I booked us a few author appearances and book signings for next year, making sure he could get the time off work. Pfft. No big deal. We'll just keep playing this game until people forget about my book, or I publish a new one, whichever comes sooner. Putting on a show for the reading public is easy.

Putting on a show for my family? Well. That's a horse of a different color.

Six months after that fateful day in the theater, I'm suppressing the urge to kick myself. Hard.

Under the table, because otherwise my parents might notice.

My dad is one of those guys who always looks like a doctor. It doesn't matter what he's wearing, you can't help but picture him in a white coat and a stethoscope. My mom slightly less so, but that's mostly because of the celebratory nose stud she got after my baby sister was born. They're actually both doctors; my dad specializes in internal medicine, and my mom specializes in podiatry. They both specialize in a total inability to seem interested in my life.

"It's so nice to see you again," my mom says to Dean for the third time. "Now, I'm sorry, you'll have to remind me - what line of work did you say you're in?"

"Murders and executions, mostly," I mutter under my breath. But apparently my mother hasn't started losing her hearing yet.

"What's that, honey?" she asks mildly, poking at

her plain steamed fillet of fish.

I shake my head, immediately regretting it. "Nothing, Mom. Just a joke."

"I want to know the joke!" She takes a sip of her wine.

"It's from a movie," says Dean helpfully. "*American Psycho.*"

"Oh," my mom intones. "What's that about?"

"A successful businessman who's also a serial killer," I tell her.

"Oh no! That's terrible." She tsks, taking another suspicious look at her fish. "Why would anyone make a movie about that?"

My dad sighs. "It's not a true story, Bea. Just a horror movie. You don't have to act so shocked."

"It's a comedy, actually," Dean puts in.

I kick his shin under the table. Not hard, but enough to make a point.

"What's so funny about killing people?" My mom knits her eyebrows, shaking her head at me. "I swear, I never understood your sense of humor."

"Anyway, the joke is that Felicity has no idea *what* I do," Dean says, patting my hand. "Just that I'm in 'business.' And really, that's good enough. The details are boring. I don't even like talking about it."

"Oh, busy businessman!" My mom's already gone through most of the bottle of wine, and she hasn't even started on her entrée yet. Probably because it's slightly more exotic than unflavored oatmeal, and she hasn't quite decided what to make of it. "Good for you. Felicity was always so artsy, I figured she'd end up with somebody like her."

Artsy. It's her nice way of saying scatterbrained. She wasn't too happy about my brothers going into mechanical trades, but at least it was something practical.

Thankfully, my oldest sister took the pressure off all of us by showing the proper amount of interest in medicine from a young age. While I drew epic cartoon stories and my brothers tried to take apart the lawn mower, my sister played "hospital" with all her dolls lined up in makeshift toilet paper bandages. Predictably, she loved biology in high school, and before long she was accepted into a prestigious medical school and well on her way to the only career path my parents truly understand.

For me, "become a doctor" was only a slightly less realistic goal than "build a homestead on Mars." I was simply missing whatever gene Tabby has, the one that's gratified by studying diseases and muscle groups and the names of all the tiny bones in your ear.

I love my family. I do. But after a lifetime of being the inexplicable middle child, the one my parents always mentioned last when they caught up with friends and extended family - *"oh, Felicity, she's just...she's still showing a lot of interest in telling stories, so we're hoping she'll take up journalism or technical writing, you know? But the most important thing is that she's happy..."*

I'm just over it.

They're proud of me, of course. But I still always feel like I'm on the other side of the glass at the zoo, and while they gawk and appreciate, they'll never understand.

"It's so romantic, the story of how you two got together," my mother says, a little dreamily. When my father gives her a sharp look, she rolls her eyes. "Don't worry, I won't bring up anything embarrassing. I skimmed over those parts anyway."

"It's not *all* based on fact," I point out, suddenly feeling a hot blush creeping up the back of my neck. I've managed to avoid thinking about my mother reading sex scenes I wrote, but the look on her face tells me that she might not be completely truthful about the "skimming" thing.

"Stop it," my dad mutters. "You're embarrassing her."

It's tempting to face-plant into my lasagna, but somehow, I resist the urge.

CHAPTER THREE

Master

We're finally home, after the longest two hours of my life.

By which I mean, of course, that *I'm* home. I didn't even live here when I was with Dean, but it's all too easy to fall into old mindsets all the same.

"I don't think I can handle another dinner with your mom wondering if my penis is shaped like the guy in the book," he mutters, raking his hands through his hair.

"I'm *sure* she was not doing that," I insist. "Probably."

Dean groans, flopping back on the sofa. "I'm really starting to regret saying I would do this. Can't we invent some kind of emergency that sends me out of town?"

Glaring at him, I sprawl on the lounge chair across

the room. "Are you really giving me a hard time? This is the least you can do."

"Fuck's sake, Lissy." He scrubs his hands across his face. "Don't start this again. I'm happy to be here. Really. I'm happy to help you out. I know what you think about me these days, but..."

He drifts off, gazing at the floor, seeming to think better of whatever he was about to say.

"But?" I prompt him, tone softening slightly.

"But I still care about you," he says, glancing at me. "You were the most important person in my life for five years, I can't just throw that away."

And now I'm not the most important person in anybody's life.

The thought comes, unwelcome, and I can't seem to push it aside.

Sighing, I curl up, drawing my knees into my chest. "Well, that's nice." I'm honestly not quite sure if I'm being sarcastic.

"And I know you care about me, too," he prompts. "Because otherwise you would've just hired a gigolo."

A burst of laughter escapes before I can stop it. "Shit. I could've written that off as research, probably."

"Sure. Tell the IRS you're hiring hookers. What could go wrong?" Dean shrugs, and it all comes back in a rush. The sadness, the regret. I remember now why I loved him so much. We had that rapport. We just got along so well - like two people who were meant to be together.

Too bad he turned out to be a liar and a cheater and a general, all-purpose scumbag.

I still can't reconcile what I *know* about Dean with the man sitting in front of me. It's never made sense to me.

I've never quite accepted it, never been able to wrap my head all the way around his betrayal.

It's not like him.

I'm letting his unasked question - *do* I still care about him? - linger in the air. I don't know the answer, and I don't want to. Of course I still care about him as a human being, more or less. I'd drag him out of a burning building just as readily as I'd drag anyone else. Maybe because I'm too compassionate, or maybe, just maybe...

No. I can't let myself have doubts. Not now. The past is the past, and if he was innocent, then why did he leave? Innocent people don't walk away from relationships like that. He had "guilty conscience" written all over him.

Goddamn it. I want to forget. After all this time, there's still a part of me that wants to just crawl over to the sofa and curl up in his arms. Pretend that I've forgotten everything that's come between us. I just want to feel him breathing, hear his heartbeat.

I want to make love. Maybe it wasn't always the best sex in the world, but at least it felt like it meant something. Even if that was a lie, I didn't know back then. It seemed real. It seemed *right*.

Warden, don't do this now.
Get yourself together.
Any day now.

After Dean goes to bed, I finally feel brave enough to check my phone again. I know M's going to be mad, that's a given. The only question is why I care so much.

It's just a silly game. That's all. It's fun, it's an escape, and it's completely harmless. I can stop anytime I want to.

Right.

He only sent me two messages after I started ignoring him earlier.

M: Lana?

And then:

M: ?

Two messages in four hours, that means he's pissed for sure. I should just ignore it. I should delete this damn anonymous messaging app, block him on every social media profile I have, and move on with my life. Instead, I text him back.

I had to go to dinner.

It takes me a few tries to delete the "sorry" from the beginning of the message. He doesn't need an apology. I haven't done anything wrong. But I still feel like I ought to apologize, and I don't know why.

M: Really?

What?

M: You know how I feel about being ignored.

I told you. I was busy.

M: You're always busy. That shouldn't get in the way of our arrangement. How long have we been doing this, Lana?

I don't know.

M: Four months, Lana. Every day, for four months now, I've spent at least a little bit of my time thinking about how to shock you. Surprise you. Pleasure you. And this is the thanks I get.

You know my situation.

M: You always made plenty of time for me before.

I want to say something else, to make up more excuses, but my stomach's already in knots over it. You see, M thinks my book is a true story. Like everyone else, he thinks me and "Damien" are actually a couple. He thinks I'm in love, committed, deeply attached to another man. And yet he's happy to do this with me.

Scumbag.

It's amazing how much I don't care, when he says just the right thing to turn me on. It's amazing how little it matters, when it's just about sex. But it's starting to feel like more than that.

Keep it together, Warden.

I'm so starved for a meaningful emotional attachment with another human being, I'm actually starting to...

I can't. It's *M*. For fuck's sake.

I finally respond.

I'm not making any more excuses. Take it or leave it.

M: Doesn't work like that.

What the hell does *that* mean?

I think it works however I want it to work.

M: Wrong. That's not why you're doing this.

Oh, really? Why don't you tell me more about my private thoughts and motivations. I'm fascinated.

M: You have to play the competent entrepreneur in your real life, and you do it well, but it scares you. It's all new. It's nothing you were ever prepared for. What if you fuck up? All the responsibility is on your head. You need a place to go and rid yourself of all that responsibility. A place where someone tells you to jump, and all you have to do is ask how high. You need a release. And you think I'm the man to give it to you.

I blink at the screen a few times.

You're nuts.

M: Search your feelings, you know it to be true.

I love it when you talk nerdy to me.

M: Take off your panties.

Why should I?

M: Because you want to. But you need someone to give you permission.

God, I hate him.

You don't know anything about what I want.

M: If only that were true. You think I enjoy dealing with you and your bratty attitude? It's basically charity work. I'm compelled to help you like the good Samaritan I am. That man of yours certainly isn't scratching that itch.

This is the first time he's directly referenced Damien. There's a sour taste in my mouth, but I'm still throbbing between my legs.

Because he's right. I want it. I want all of it. I don't even know *what* I want, and that's the point. He knows, so I don't have to. How does he have that power over me?

Obviously it's just my mind playing tricks on me. What I *really* want is to follow orders, and he's just exceptionally good at giving them. He's inside my head, convincing me of my own desires so seamlessly that my libido can't even tell the difference.

I feel a little bit lightheaded. As I unbutton my jeans, another message comes in.

M: Don't touch yourself.

Damn it.

Not only has he anticipated my next move, he's aware that I'm already following his orders without having to be told again. I hate being a foregone conclusion. I hate how well he knows me, better than I know myself.

How is that even possible?

More importantly: How am I going to function with another human being up in my space? Dean is sleeping just a few feet away, through a way-too-thin wall. I keep reminding myself that I just need to get through my parents' visit, but those two weeks are going to feel like an eternity. M's influence over my life has grown so gradually, weaving itself into every moment, every breath, that I didn't realize how insidious it was until now.

I step out of my panties and shove them into the hamper before shimmying back into my jeans. The fabric rasping against my sensitive flesh is uncomfortable, but in a really nice way. I glance at myself in the mirror - my face flushed, eyes so dilated they look black. My heart races, and I feel like I'm balanced on a razor's edge.

Almost like I could...

I tap out a message to M.

I need to know if I have your permission.

M: Are you that close?

I think so.

M: You have my permission to come, so long as you don't use your hands. Or anything else. Just squeeze those gorgeous thighs together and rock into the feeling.

I sit down on the edge of the bed. Now that I know I'm allowed to, a rush of arousal leaves me weak-kneed and quivering. I close my eyes and follow his instructions, slowly rocking back and forth so that the stiff seam of the fabric rubs where I need it most.

My phone buzzes and I force my eyes open again.

M: You'll never come again without thinking of me.

When the pleasure explodes, low in my belly, I curse softly. I'm cursing at him even though he can't hear me.

I'm determined to prove him wrong, though a part of me fears he's not.

CHAPTER FOUR

The Wager

Jack is laughing at me, over the phone. "You're a national treasure, do you know that? Please never stop making terrible decisions for my entertainment."

I scowl. "I wouldn't be in this mess in the first place if you'd just agreed to help me out."

"This again." He's still laughing. "I promise you, the mess would've been a thousand times worse with me involved. I'm also a walking disaster; the difference is that I know how to avoid the situations that are gonna make it worse. You're better off with Shithead. Just don't fall in love with him again."

"Right," I snort.

"Don't laugh," he warns. "Much smarter people than you have done much stupider things."

"Thanks," I groan. "Great pep talk."

"I'm just trying to nip this in the bud. You fell in love with him for a reason, and you're gonna start remembering those reasons the more time you spend with him. You're gonna start forgetting all the very good reasons why you ended it, and then you're going to put your mouth on his mouth..."

"None of that is going to happen," I promise him. "This isn't you and Christine all over again."

"Shhh!" he hisses. "Don't invoke her. For fuck's sake, woman."

"I am over him. Trust me," I tell him. "And more importantly than that, he's over me. *He's* the one who left, remember?"

"I'm just saying," Jack replies, mildly. "If you were over him, you would've moved on."

Of course, he defines *moving on* a little differently than I do. It's true I haven't really dated anyone since Dean left, but that doesn't mean I'm still in love with him.

"For your information," I blurt out before I can stop myself, "I *have* moved on."

"You mean the epic drought has ended, and you didn't see fit to tell your bestest friend about it?" he drawls. "I'm hurt."

"Occasionally, I like to keep things to myself," I tell him, forcing my tone to sound casual. I haven't breathed a word of this M situation to anyone, naturally, and it's making my pulse pound just thinking about it. "It's a very informal thing. I couldn't ask him to lie to my family for me. That's why I called Dean. Also, because you're no fun."

There's a few muffled clanking noises on Jack's

end. He's probably trying to figure out a way to make ramen more interesting, as usual.

"You know why Dean agreed to do this, right?" he says, finally.

"Because he feels guilty."

"Wrong," Jack replies, right before a loud clanking sound almost deafens me. "*Ow*. It's because he still loves you, idiot."

I roll my eyes at no one. "Sure. That makes a lot of sense."

"Think about it," Jack says. "You're not going to ask your boy-toy to do it, because you know he won't. Because he's not in love with you. And I wouldn't do it, because I don't indulge in total fucking insanity for friends, no matter how much endless entertainment they provide. That's something you only do if you love somebody like you're in a damn Nicholas Sparks book. I'm not saying he's trying to win you back, but nobody thinks this kind of thing is a good idea unless there are some serious hormones in play."

One of Jack's more charming qualities is that he always believes he's right. Sometimes he actually is, but this isn't one of those situations. He never met Dean. He didn't see how things fell apart, the way Dean's eyes went empty, whatever light had drawn me to him in the first place slowly extinguishing.

"You could not be more wrong," I inform him.

He just chuckles. "Mark my words, Warden."

Before I knew my parents were planning a visit, I agreed to do a book signing downtown during the same week. Of course, they wanted to come and see all the excitement. I promised them it would be boring to hang out there for hours if they weren't actually interested in getting autographs from the signing authors. But they demurred and insisted, so here we are.

Dean acts as my assistant, but everyone knows why he's really here, and everybody wants to meet him. He plays the part so well, smiling and ducking his eyes down when people pay him ridiculous compliments. Most of them are just very sweet, but a few of them brush a little too close to flirting. I mean, I don't really care, but *they* don't know that. They think we're together. It twists in my stomach a little; how can people be so brazen?

The longest line in the room is for Adrian Risinger's table. Of course. I can't see him very well from this side of the room, but I can see the six-foot-tall banner advertising his presence. He's always the celebrity at these things, one of the few male romance authors who's revealed his true identity:former CEO, current billionaire, and basically the only reason he comes to these things is pure ego. It's irritating on principle, even though all his book sales go to charity.

But now that I see him interacting with his fans, how engaging and genuine he seems, and how they're all glowing when they walk away from his table - a grudging respect starts to form in the back of my mind.

There's a social hour for the authors after this, and I don't really expect Adrian to show up. I managed to get passes for my parents to attend, and my mom's sipping champagne and giggling to herself while my dad just surveys the room and tries to figure out what the hell is going on.

"*All those people* wanted to see you!" my mother

marvels as Dad rolls his eyes.

"She already told you how many thousands of copies she sold, how is this more impressive?" he grumbles.

Mom shakes her head stubbornly. "I don't know. It's just different when you can actually see their faces." She beams at me. "How are you handling it, honey? I know you're not such a big fan of being social."

"She's great with them," Dean cuts in, handing me something that I hope to God has a high alcohol content. I take a sip and make a face. Not high enough. But it'll do.

"Very gracious, they absolutely love her," he goes on.

"Not as much as they love you," I tell him, with a forced smile. "How does it feel to be a rockstar?"

"Pretty damn good!" he says cheerfully. He's refusing to pick up on my subtext. Which is a positive thing if I'm mostly concerned about people buying the lie, but slightly less so if I'm trying not to kill him.

There's a little murmur from one end of the room, attracting my parents' attention. At least that reduces the risk of them noticing the steam pouring out of my ears. A moment later, I realize what the cause of the commotion is.

Adrian Risinger just walked in.

I didn't get a good look at him before, but I certainly do now. He's a tall drink of water, with dirty-blond hair, expensively cut, and a neatly trimmed beard. He's slightly too handsome for real life, but only *slightly*. There's something about him that's sharp, I can't quite put my finger on it - not his clothes in particular, not his features really, but an overall quality that makes me want to sit up a little straighter and listen to what he has to say.

The voluptuous redhead beside him is also tall, I

realize after a moment - just not nearly as tall as he is, but she'd almost stand eye-to-eye with Dean, and her heels aren't *that* high. I have to admit that I'm surprised. About the curves, not the height. My heart twinges a little to see a man like him with a woman like her. I know it happens, in theory, but *seeing* it is an entirely different thing. When I used to go out with Dean, I felt like everyone was staring. Wondering. *What the hell does he see in her? Was she skinny when they got together?*

There's no room for wondering with Mr. Risinger's girlfriend. I can picture him falling in love with her. *I'm* a little bit in love with her. It helps that he's obviously still smitten, smiling and glancing at her and showing no indication he's aware of anyone else in the room.

He shakes a few hands when people manage to get his attention, but he's clearly making his way towards the bar, and therefore towards us.

"Who's that?" my mom hisses, her eyes nearly bugging out of her head.

"Adrian Risinger," I murmur, keeping him in my peripheral view. Is he actually going to come talk to me? "He's a real-life billionaire who writes romance novels about billionaires."

"*What?*" My dad looks like his head's about to explode. And not in a good way, like my mom's.

"Lana," says a voice, and I turn around to see Adrian's girlfriend approaching me rapidly. "It's so great to finally meet you! I loved your book."

"Thank you." I sort of gape at her for a second as she shakes my hand.

"I'm Meg," she informs me.

"Right," I say. "Of course. The muse."

Adrian smiles, flanking her. "And then some."

Meg's eyebrows jump slightly, in a way that tells me that he *probably* just grabbed her ass. The body language fits. It's a bold move in a room with so many glances wandering in their direction. I'd be pretty pissed if Dean ever did that to me in public, even at our closest.

"It's not as glamorous as it sounds," says Meg, and Adrian's eyes suddenly widen as her arm slides behind his back. "Trust me."

She returned the favor. Because, of *course* she did.

"Tell me about it," says Dean, and a sudden understanding dawns on Meg's face. She untangles herself from her lover and steps towards my fictional one.

"So you're the famous Damien," she says, shaking his hand with a smile. She's referring to him by his book-name, of course. I'm still not quite used to that. "Well done."

"Way to raise the bar," says Adrian. "We're all fucked now."

"Let's face it, *you* were fucked in comparison to most serial killers," says Meg. "And some of the lesser demons."

He winks at her.

"You're welcome," says Dean, grinning. The urge to roll my eyes is powerful, but we're supposed to be *in love*. Then again, Meg and Adrian are very obviously *in love*, and also very obviously balanced on a knife's edge of biting sarcasm that seems like it might suddenly tumble into something that's very inappropriate for a public setting.

I'm insanely jealous.

This is, if I'm being perfectly honest with myself, the kind of relationship I could picture having with M. Not that I do. Not that I ever *would*. But they look so happy.

You don't know him.

But it doesn't feel that way. It never really has. I suspect I know him better than I ever knew Dean, at any rate.

I shake my head in a valiant effort to dismiss the insanity that seems to have taken hold. I have to pull myself together. Once this whole mess is over, I'm breaking things off with M. Right now I need it for my sanity, because it's the only part of my life that makes any kind of sense. But after I've managed to delicately end the situation between me and Dean, and convince my family that I'm not dying of a broken heart, I'm moving the fuck on.

At least I learned something from him. Now, I know what I want, and I can go after it. He's hardly the only dominant man in the world, and I doubt he's even the one I mesh with the best. Right? I mean, what are the odds?

After I introduce Meg and Adrian to my parents, we say a few polite goodbyes and the power couple starts making their rounds in the room. I meet a few more authors, some I've heard of and many more I haven't, and Dean charms every single person he meets.

I almost forgot how charismatic he could be. The first time he walked up to me in the park, I was sure it was the setup for a prank reality show. Guys like him don't go after girls like me.

Except, of course, when they do.

We'd passed each other plenty of times before. I'd noticed him, of course, the way you notice handsome well-dressed men when they cross your path. But I never expected to look up and see him sitting down beside me on the bench, offering me a snack-size apple pie.

"They gave me an extra one," he said with a grin. "Figured I might as well share it with somebody."

I'd like to say it took me a couple of weeks of cautious, demure flirting and casual coffee dates. But he asked me out for dinner that night, and I said yes. It was wonderful. I had just enough wine to get a little giddy, and I kissed him in my front hallway until I could hardly catch my breath.

He said he'd noticed me, too. The books I was reading on my lunch break, the way the wind ruffled my chestnut-brown hair. After Andrew, I meant to be cautious. I wasn't going to let myself fall too fast and too deep. I had to keep my wits about me.

I invited Dean in for coffee after our third date. Never got around to making that coffee, but he did spend the night. From that moment, I never hesitated, never doubted, and never looked back.

After two back-to-back betrayals, I really am starting to wonder what the hell is wrong with me. Not that it's my fault, per se, but I must be doing something to attract these types. What is it about me that beckons to the liars, the cheaters, the emotional vampires who feed off of my blind devotion?

Plenty of people would say it's my waistline, but I refuse to accept that. Maybe I'm an easy target because I still have soft curves where so many other women have sleek, tanned skin and lean muscle. But look at Meg. Sure, her boyfriend can obviously be a bit of a pill, but I saw the way he looked at her. She practically has him on a leash. As much as I'd like to bitterly predict the inevitable demise of their relationship, I can't even lie to myself.

So what is it about me? What vibes am I putting out into the world that say, "please, betray me! Please lie to me!" It can't just be a coincidence.

I'm staring blankly at the picked-over offerings on the buffet table when I notice Meg and Adrian having a slightly hushed conversation in the little recessed doorway area behind it. I'm not trying to listen, but they're not trying that hard to be quiet, either.

"It's indecent," she's saying.

"*You're* indecent," he replies fervently, glancing over his shoulder before he steals a kiss. "You know what would go really well with this dress? That flush you get across your chest when I make you -"

"*Stop* it," she insists. "You're not playing fair."

"Oh, *I'm* the one who's not playing fair?" From the sound of his voice, I suspect he's raised an eyebrow at her. "So the push-up bra was just a coincidence."

"Not everything is because of you. Ego-maniac. I like to dress nicely for the fans." There's a smirk in her voice. "You're so going to lose, by the way."

"So you keep saying. And yet I remain unmoved."

"I wouldn't say *that*," Meg laughs softly. "By the way, have you noticed we're in a hotel?"

"I might have."

The temptation to look up in the ensuing silence is too great. She's pressing a key card into his hand, and he's standing there with slowly widening eyes.

"If you feel like surrendering, meet me there in the next half-hour," she purrs. Then, she turns abruptly on her heel and starts walking away from him.

Right towards me.

I try to adopt a casual stance, gazing somewhere into the middle distance, but she pauses as she passes by me.

"Word of advice," she mutters, grabbing a small pastry and devouring it with all the fervor I imagine she wants to devour him. "If you're thinking it might be fun to do one of those 'who can go longer without sex' wagers, *it's not*."

I almost burst out laughing, but I'm conscious of Adrian still standing not too far away from me. "Why...?"

"Because I thought I could *win*," she says. "Easily. Now look at me, I'm resorting to guerrilla tactics. And he's completely merciless. Do you know he's worn nothing but button-down jeans around the house for the last three days? And I do mean *nothing*." She shoots a brief, baleful glance in his direction. "And it's driven me to the point of insanity where I'm just blabbering to a stranger about my sex life."

"Your secret's safe with me," I assure her. "I think you've got him. Stay strong. For womankind."

She snorts with laughter. "Thanks, but no promises. I'd better go."

"Good luck," I call after her, and a moment later, Adrian passes by, grabbing a handful of small cookies without slowing in his stride.

"No fair taking sides," he says through clenched teeth. "You have no idea what I've been through."

It's not until later that night, when I'm getting ready for bed, that I finally get around to checking my phone again. There's only one message in the app.

M: New rule. When you want me, you are to drop your panties on the floor, take a picture, and send it to me. Otherwise I won't respond.

In spite of myself, I just smirk. Nobody could ever accuse him of being anything but straightforward. And right now, that's exactly what I need.

Yes, Sir.

He doesn't answer. I drift off to sleep with my phone resting on my stomach and my hand on top of that, just in case.

CHAPTER FIVE

A Decent Proposal

Dean

Lissy just so happens to have a meeting with her agent the same week her parents are visiting. One to which I'm not invited. Of course. It all seems a little bit too convenient, but I'm not arguing with her. Of course Lissy would never lie about her whereabouts just to get a little time to herself. Lissy sits in flawless judgment of all those around her.

Bitter? Why would I be bitter? After five years, to have her turn on me like a rabid dog - I don't care if you literally catch somebody with their dick out, you don't go cold like that. Not with somebody you love. It's not possible. You think I haven't been hurt before? Betrayed?

Well, I fucking have. And I could never just flip that switch. I wish it was that simple, believe me.

The instant she decided on her version of the truth, there was no hope for me. She was done with me. Her heart turned to stone, or maybe it always was, and that was just the moment I realized it.

Of course I knew about Andrew. That's why things got so out of hand in the first place. She told me all about that scumbag on our second date, eyes going glassy over a giant salad that she didn't even want to eat, that she only ordered because she didn't want to look "like a pig." (Her words, not mine.) She apologized a thousand times, said she knew how obnoxious it was to hear about somebody's ex, but she just needed to get it off her chest. Needed me to understand why she was a little skittish.

Well, who wouldn't be? Let's be honest, these days cheating is a garden-variety offense in relationships. But most people don't make a point of shoving it in their partner's face. Andrew was a champion at that. He turned the other woman into the purloined letter, the betrayal that was so obvious it couldn't be a real betrayal. Because if he wanted to cheat, surely he'd do it behind Lissy's back. And Lissy, ever accommodating, ever wanting to be the *cool girlfriend*, made the biggest mistake of her life.

She trusted him.

And then, one day, like something out of a Biz Markie song, she found out that other girl wasn't "just a friend."

It shattered her world, but she thought she'd managed to pick up all the pieces. I could tell otherwise.

I only lied to protect her, but that's always a piss-poor excuse when all the cards are on the table. But what other choice did I have?

Maybe I was selfish. Maybe I deserved it. Maybe I should've done everything differently. Hell, maybe I never should have walked up to her in the first place.

It was the way she always looked, sitting on that bench. At first she'd be self-conscious, glancing around her, shoulders slightly hunched, willing people not to look at her. But then she'd start to read, and slowly, she'd forget where she was. Her face would light up, and every time I walked past her I had this feeling like I was seeing something special. Something most people were missing. She had such a pretty smile when she thought nobody was looking.

Once I actually started talking to her, I realized a lot more. She was smart. Whip-smart. Too smart for the temp agency she was working at, and probably too smart for me. I asked her to be my girlfriend anyway, and within a few months she'd moved into my place.

From there, things were good. Most of the time, they were great. We dealt with the usual tensions that couples do, but after a while, it seemed like we were both comfortably settled in. Sometimes she seemed a little distant during sex, but she always said everything was okay.

I should've known. The first time I picked up that book of hers, just morbidly curious and wondering if maybe she'd put a villain in there who was based on me -

Oh, there was a girl between these pages that I'd never known. Of course authors aren't their characters, or their books, except in this case she was. They had the same name. It was "based on a true story." I was pretty much one hundred percent sure it actually wasn't, but I work in marketing. I'm certainly not going to throw stones.

Lana was Lissy, down to the way she talked, the thoughts she had, and - I'd bet my life on it - the fantasies. Within a few hours of meeting him, Lana's fantasizing about Damien bending her over the desk. And not just to fuck her. To spank her.

Okay, so there's always room for a little playful tap in the bedroom, but that's not what this was. She wanted to be spanked, and spanked *hard*, as a punishment. As some kind of masochistic sexual release. I know that's a common enough theme in these books, but I guess I didn't realize how commonplace it was in real life until I started looking into it. Damn, but there are a lot of women out there who crave a firm hand.

And Lissy's one of them. I can tell by the detailed, loving way she writes about it. Her descriptions of the beautiful rope bondage aren't quite as evocative, so I figure that one's a little lower down on her priority list. But Lana loves taking orders. Being made to crawl across the floor, carrying things in her mouth, all the while glaring and yowling and practically spitting at his feet. She's got that love-hate thing down pat. She hates this guy, but she's dripping wet for him.

These are Lissy's fantasies. Everything I never knew about her, all the things that ran through her head when she was alone in the tub. Meanwhile, with me, she'd happily roll onto her back for some sweet but generally uninspired missionary position - and hell, it wouldn't surprise me if she was faking it. There's all kinds of things in the back of her mind that I don't know, that I'll never know.

Why didn't she just tell me?

I was angry about that for a while, but I guess it makes sense. When your fantasy's for someone to manhandle and punish you, to be in charge, it's hard to negotiate for that. But I could've done it. I would've done anything for her.

Of course, I realize that's not what she wanted, either. Somebody just appeasing her needs. That's not part of the fantasy. I would've had to want it too, and maybe she was afraid of finding out that I didn't.

Well, I'll admit that I *used* to be pretty vanilla. These days, though? I like to think I could show a kinky girl a good time.

Admittedly, I haven't tried. Clubs are intimidating, and the meat market online is pretty disheartening too. I guess I've got the same fantasy everybody else does, of just meeting someone out in the wild whose interests just happen to perfectly align with yours.

Maybe I was Dom material all along. I've always been a good leader, and now I manage fifteen people under me in my department. I know how to act like a boss, and that seems like about ninety percent of the arrangement. I mean, didn't Adrian Risinger's submissive secretary fall in love with him in real life? That's probably not a coincidence.

And that's the other interesting thing. I always assumed submissives were, well, *submissive*. All the time. But Meg walks into a room like she owns it. Maybe that was why I never suspected a thing about Lissy. When we met, she was self-sufficient, and had managed to pick herself up and keep pushing forward after a nasty breakup. It wasn't until we were in the bedroom that her bashfulness came out. I should've known.

The sound of my phone jars me out of my thoughts. It's a text message, from Lissy's mom. We'd exchanged numbers years ago at some holiday get-together or other, but she never actually contacted me until now.

I know Lissy is busy, but Ted and I were hoping you could join us for lunch. Our little secret. :)

So, basically there's a few options here. Either I'm going to get there and find out that Ted was "busy" and this is some kind of twisted Mrs. Robinson thing, or...I'm not sure what the second option is, actually. I'm pretty sure it's not the first one, though.

Lissy would kill me if she found out I'm meeting with her parents alone - too easy to get the story mixed up - but I *have* to know what they've got in mind. I'll just make sure to establish an out for myself if things get too weird.

What's the worst that could happen?

"Sorry I can't stay long," I tell Bea and Ted as I slide into my seat at the mildly upscale midtown bistro. "You know I told my boss about this a month ago, but there was some client meeting they just couldn't reschedule."

"We understand," says Ted. "You know, Bea, we could always talk about this another time."

"Oh, no no no!" Bea cuts in. I silently agree with her. "Don't be silly. This won't take long. We'll have it figured out before the entrées come."

The curiosity is killing me.

"*So*," says Bea, leaning closer to me. There's a look in her eyes that I really, really don't like. "How long have you two been together, then?"

My mind races for the fake timeline we invented. It couldn't be too long, because then it would apparently "annoy them" that I hadn't proposed yet. Thankfully I spent our first few holidays as a couple with my own family, so they're not going to notice any discrepancies there. "Um...three years," I blurt out. "Or thereabouts. Lissy's better at remembering the specifics."

Thank God for that ancient stereotype about men not remembering anniversaries. I can coast on this one. Bea's mind is already racing ahead to something else, and I have a feeling I'm not going to like it.

"Any idea when you're going to take the next step?" She's trying very hard to be lighthearted and friendly about it, but there's always something accusatory about this question. I take a deep breath.

"I mean, you know, it's a lot. Big decision. We'd have to talk about it first, I'm not the kind of guy to just...you know, spring it out of nowhere."

"Well, she wants you to," says Bea confidentially. "I was just talking to her about it yesterday."

She has to be lying, but I try to reel in my incredulous tone. "Really? She *said* that?"

Bea makes a non-committal gesture. "You have to read between the lines. A girl like Felicity doesn't always say what's on her mind. Sometimes it takes a mother's intuition."

She taps the side of her nose, and I just nod, slowly. Lissy doesn't really bite her tongue around me. She never did.

"So." Bea touches my hand. "I know it's a lot, I know it's scary, and you probably don't even know where to start. But that's okay. I'm going to help you. We'll plan something amazing that she's never going to forget."

That's for damn sure.

"Uh," I stall, still trying to wrap my head around what's happening. "I don't know if..."

"Well, are you planning to marry her or not?" Bea's voice has gone sharp. "If you're not in this for the long haul, I don't think you should be playing games with her."

"That's not the point," I insist, wanting desperately to just tell her to butt out. But I know I can't. At minimum, I have to keep things civil to avoid any drama, and it's starting to seem like I'll have to do a lot more than that. "It's something very personal, and very -"

"No." Bea shakes her head. "It's not personal, because you don't just marry a *person*. You marry a family. It would've been more ideal to do this during one of the holidays when everybody's already together, but we missed our chance. The good news is, I've talked to some of the kids. Most of them will be able to make it down here within the next few weeks. I'll just tell Felicity we're doing an impromptu family reunion of sorts, because there was a sale on airfare or something. Meanwhile, you and I can plan the big moment." Her eyes are shining as she practically bounces out of her seat with excitement. "Oh, this is going to be so beautiful. She'll be thrilled."

Fuck.

"Uh, I guess I could start looking at rings," I say, slowly. I have a bad feeling I'm going to regret this, but what the hell else can I do?

"Excellent!" she beams. "Get the ring, plan the speech. Just leave the rest up to me. When the time is right, I'll let you know."

Lissy is *definitely* going to murder me.

"Do you know something about this?"

Lissy is waving her phone in my face accusatorially. What the fuck, did she already find out? Is she just toying with me? I blink a few times and try to focus on the screen, like I don't already know what she's talking about.

"Know something about *what*?" I think I sound suitably irritated, and therefore innocent.

She sighs sharply. "Mom is bringing the whole fam-damily into town. I am *so* not equipped to deal with this right now. My brothers are going to be here on the same weekend we're supposed to go to that writers and readers fetish ball. How am I supposed to explain that?"

I shrug. "Just tell them you've got a prior work commitment. You're not obligated to show them your corset and heels."

Lissy rolls her eyes, and I hope it's not because she'd never dream of wearing a corset and heels. Because I'd be lying if I said I didn't want to see that.

"Relax. It'll be fine," I tell her. "By the way, what am I supposed to wear to that thing?"

"Same thing all guys wear to these parties. Leather pants, leather gloves, leather everything." She's got her head buried in the fridge as she searches for something, so I can't read her expression to see if she's fantasizing about anything in particular.

"Sounds sticky," I observe.

"You'll want some baby powder," she agrees. "Leather pants at minimum. The kind with the lace-up fly."

"*That* sounds like a pain in the ass." I shake my

head. "I'm going with a zipper."

Her head pops up. "Trust me," she says. "Laces. Otherwise you might as well be wearing jeans."

"Yes ma'am." I grin, getting up from the sofa. "How was the meeting?"

"Just a lot of contract stuff." She straightens, holding two beers. "These are both for me, by the way."

"Thanks," I tell her, reaching past her for another one. "Any other fetish ball tips? Is it a faux pas to wear underwear?"

"You'll probably regret it if you don't," she smirks. "But you won't be able to stuff a pair of boxers under leather pants - not if they fit right. Get some decent briefs."

"Define decent."

"Not in a three-pack from a big box store," she says, going to the cupboard.

"I'm kind of offended that you feel the need to say that," I inform her. "I'm a boss now. I dress for success."

"Yeah, well your employees aren't seeing your underwear, I hope." She examines a can of soup. "Although, of course someone else might..."

She's referring to Jessica, of course.

I'm not dignifying that with a response. She can think whatever she wants to think, it doesn't make a difference to me. We're done. I gave her five years of my life, and she couldn't learn to trust me.

Never again.

CHAPTER SIX

The Gang's All Here

Lizzy

"Hey, hey, the gang's all here!" my mom cries out, and she runs to my older sister Tabby for a hug. We're all crowded around baggage claim at LaGuardia, wishing for the floor to open up and swallow us whole. Or maybe that's just me.

Tabby comes to me next, squeezing me tight before she pulls back to look me up and down. "I'm so happy for you," she enthuses. "Finally found the one!"

"Guess there's hope for all of us," says little sister Stephanie, continuing the grand family tradition of the back-handed compliment.

My brothers all hug me, then slap Dean on the

back in quick succession. He looks slightly off-balance by the end of it, which affords me a little private smile.

Dean's an only child, and over the years, he and his parents have grown distant. He never seemed to adjust to the dynamics of a big, loud family when he spent holidays with us, and I can't believe he took the news of their visit so well. It almost seemed like he was prepared for it, which doesn't make any sense. Why would my parents have told him about it before me?

"I heard there's this amazing undiscovered seafood place uptown," my middle brother Scott says. "Hey Dean, do you think you can leverage some of those business connections to get us in?"

"I promise you, Scott, if you've heard of it, it's not undiscovered." I smile at him. "Also, don't you think it's a little too early to be asking for favors?"

"Hey, he's part of the family now!" Big brother Nick slaps Dean on the back. "Seriously though, don't listen to anything Scott says."

"Boys," my dad says, sounding bored. "Please."

"I can get you into any restaurant you like," says Dean with a dazzling smile.

Right. I forgot he could charm people. Even my sister Tabby, who is several magnitudes more gorgeous than I am and is married to a pilot with steel-blue eyes, can't stop staring at him.

Not that I can really blame her. When he first walked up to me in that park, I thought it was some kind of prank. He looks like he should be on the cover of GQ, or at the very least, a Lexus ad. His deep brown hair is close-cropped and well-styled; he obviously goes to a more expensive barber now that he's managing a whole team at the ad agency. He's only mentioned that fact about ten times since he moved in.

His eyes are this sort of inexplicable silver-gray, which I suppose I didn't fully appreciate after years of being with him. They really are pretty striking.

Well, nobody's questioning how handsome he is. Doesn't change what he did. But I have to pretend like we're in love, so I focus on his eyes.

Uh oh. This could get dangerous.

Damn it. Jack was right. I've moved on, I'm over it. I want nothing more to do with Dean romantically. He's helping me out as a friend - admittedly a friend I don't trust as far as I can throw - but I can't stop staring at those *eyes*.

"So, Dean." Stephanie has managed to worm her way between us. "You're like Don Draper, huh?"

He laughs, way too cheerfully for the situation. "Sadly, no. I deserve neither such praise, nor such censure."

"Oh my God." Tabby elbows her way in. "Did you just quote Jane Austen? Felicity, I can't believe you kept him quiet for so long."

"Well, I did bring him to three Christmases," I point out. "But, you know..."

"...I've been busy the last few years," Dean cuts in. "So I've had to miss almost everything, unfortunately. But things should change, now that I'm..."

"The head of your own team!" my mom interrupts him. "Felicity mentioned it the other day. Congratulations! You must be so excited."

"Well, it's a lot of responsibility," he says. "But it is pretty exciting. I've got twenty accounts now, but that's all boring work stuff." He waves his hand dismissively. "What about you, Tabby - Lissy said you just went to Syria for Doctors Without Borders?"

Damn it, how did he get so good at talking to people? Was he born like that, or did he somehow teach himself to be so engaging and captivating? It seems simple, the way things always do when you watch an expert do them. But when I'm in the middle of a conversation, especially with one of my family members, it's like the part of my brain in charge of reacting to things just shuts down. And I know you're supposed to ask questions to demonstrate your interest in somebody's life, but it always feels so awkward. Like I'm quizzing them.

For Dean, it's just easy. Effortless. He has no anxiety about it, because he never thinks anything's going to go wrong.

And why would he? Nothing ever does, for him. I'm pretty sure I'm the only bad thing that's ever happened to him, and that was certainly only a hiccup.

Lunch is...loud. I somehow manage to actually sit next to my supposed boyfriend, and while Tabby sits on his left, she soon gets pulled into an argument involving Nick, Arthur, and something about cavemen and astronauts.

"Man, are you serious with that *Pride and Prejudice* shit?" I mutter, staring at my salad. "You know my sister has a thing for Mr. Darcy."

"All bookish women do," says Dean, glancing at me. "Are you trying to claim you *don't*?"

"Yeah, well, I'm immune to you now. How on earth does it still work on everyone else, though?"

"Second rule of marketing," he says, gesturing to

the server. "Play to your market."

"What's the first rule?" I have a feeling I'm going to regret asking.

He grins. "Don't make them think."

"Of course." I roll my eyes.

"Hey, I'm not saying people are stupid." Dean shrugs. "I'm just saying, there's a million things vying for their time and attention. We've all been conditioned to respond to certain triggers, certain signals, and that's the most important thing to keep in mind when you're trying to reach people. Anything they have to analyze for too long, you risk your message getting lost in translation." He picks up his drink. "Also, a *lot* of people are stupid."

"There it is. That's the man I fell in love with." I pick up my fork and examine a slice of radish. I'm pretty sure I specifically asked for no radishes, but if I bring it up, Nick's going to make a big deal out of it, and we'll probably all get free meals. Free desserts, at least. I can't handle sitting through another meal where I know the entire restaurant management hates us.

"You hate salad," Dean observes. "I remember that about you."

"I don't...hate it," I insist. "It's just that a lot of the common salad ingredients are not exactly my favorite."

"You know you have to eat like that more than once a month for it to make an actual difference," he says. "And I'm only bringing this up because I know you're torturing yourself for appearance's sake. Trust me. Nobody here would judge you if you ordered the steak that you really wanted."

I give him an irritated look. "Was it that obvious?"

"You kept flipping back to it," he says. "And then

you went for the Greek salad after all. It was quite the emotional roller coaster."

Really, there's nothing left to do but laugh. "Not much gets past you, does it?"

"Absolutely not," he says. "For instance, what's the deal with Arthur?"

Eyes widening, I glance around the table, but everyone is so absorbed in their conversations that I'm pretty sure they've forgotten I'm here.

"What do you mean?" I ask, a little too quickly.

"I mean, he hardly talks," says Dean. "I understand why you're the way you are. Middle children always have trouble finding their place."

"Thanks a lot."

"But the youngest kids..." he goes on, ignoring me. "Usually they're good at getting attention. Stephanie's got it. Arthur doesn't. So what is it about him that's different?"

I fold my arms across my chest, giving up on the salad. "You know he's right over there. He'll hear you."

"*I* can barely hear me," Dean points out. "Sorry, I figured the two misfit kids would've bonded at some point."

The truth is, I don't know what the deal is with Arthur. I've never known, and neither does anybody else. Maybe I should've made more of an effort. But these days, everyone is so scattered, and our get-togethers are, well...loud. The dominant personalities in this group, of which there is a majority, always steer the conversation and the activities.

"Try talking to him sometime," says Dean. "I know it's not your *forte*, but you're a successful author now. You should be able to talk to people. If you ever start to feel nervous, just remind yourself of your own superiority."

"That actually does not make me feel any better," I inform him. "But you're actually kind of right about Arthur, probably. And for the record, being successful hasn't helped all that much. I'm still inept at social interactions, although I have found that throwing money at people works pretty well as a social lubricant. Just not as applicable to family. Not mine, at least."

"Or cops," says Dean. "In this country. Most of the time."

Dean

I'm going for a run.

These days, I run alone. It's actually better this way. The noise of the city fades away as I do it, and I forget everything.

Usually.

But today, I can't stop thinking about Lissy. I'd almost forgotten what her family was like, how much their behavior explains almost everything about her.

Everything, that is, except her lack of trust.

That was what killed us. Not that I was perfect. I started getting lost in my work, something I never imagined I'd do - not when we were first together, and all I wanted was to see her smile.

But things started to change. Years passed, and we got comfortable with each other. Maybe too comfortable. She'd never say it out loud - she was too grateful for my paycheck - but I could tell it was starting to eat at her. I was never home. And yes, most of the time I actually *was* working. The rest of the time I was blowing off steam, meditating, the only way I know how. Pounding pavement. I know it's not good for my feet, my knees, and I know the carbon monoxide I'm inhaling is probably eating holes into my brain. Whatever. I need this. I need something, and this does it.

Lissy's family likes me, and respects me. It's not difficult for me to cultivate that. That's one of life's dirty secrets: your character doesn't matter, so long as you can fake it. Look at how many people still *voluntarily* give Jordan Belfort their money.

I'm not a scumbag, but I'm not above using their tactics. Actually proving that I'm a good person would take way too much time and effort. It's easier to smile easily, ask a lot of light questions, and laugh along with bad jokes.

Why am I doing this?

I couldn't say no to Lissy when she called. It was on the tip of my tongue, and then *yes* just popped out of my mouth.

So maybe I'm still hung up on her. Just a little bit. There was never any closure there, not that there usually is. But the way she turned on me - it never sat right.

Everything else that doesn't work out, I can just walk away from. And to my credit, I did try. But now, suddenly, here I am.

Running back to her.

Lissy

I'm sitting in a post-coital glow, staring at the screen of my phone. I wish I didn't find myself in this situation so often.

M: New rule. When we're finished, tell me "thank you, Sir."

Thank you, Sir.

That's easy enough. This isn't the first time I've found myself wondering if he actually gets off on this, like, for real - or if it's just a power trip. I don't know how he can type so quickly and so coherently if he's jerking off at the same time.

M: Good girl.

I wish that didn't give me such a warm, fuzzy feeling inside.

CHAPTER SEVEN

Leather and Laces

Dean

It's the night of the fetish ball, and Lissy managed to shake off her family for a few hours by convincing them she had a "boring literary thing." I actually did manage to find leather pants. They look...pretty good, I think. A little ridiculous, but I think the *good-ridiculous* line is one I'm cursed to walk when it comes to fetish wear.

I haven't seen Lissy's outfit yet. I have to admit I'm desperately curious. Back when we met, and she was still at the temp agency, she always looked pretty cute in her business casual clothes. After she got laid off, it was mostly jeans and sweatpants, which didn't make her any less cute. But they didn't exactly do much for her curves. She's always had this fantastic hourglass figure, which of course she thinks is "too fat" because she's not airbrushed in the mirror. My few suggestions at outfits were always shot down, and after the first time I tried to give her a sweater that hugged her chest but apparently made her stomach look "huge," I gave up.

I've managed to get myself pulled together into the pants and a nice shirt when I hear her voice coming out of the bedroom.

"Dean?"

The door's closed, but she obviously wants me to come in. Shrugging, I push it open.

Well, fuck me.

She's mostly dressed. Her leather skirt comes down mid-thigh, enough to suggest but not openly confirm that she's wearing stockings with garters. And yes, that's definitely a corset. Not some zip-up stretchy corset top, either. The real deal.

Which is, I realize, the reason why I'm here.

"Lace me up," she says calmly, gesturing to the loose ribbons hanging at her back. Well, God *damn*. She looks like a wet dream already, and it's not even properly cinched yet.

"I..." The ribbons sit there innocuously, mocking me. I'm pretty sure *my* laces just got a little tighter. "I've never done this before."

"It's just like tying shoes," she says, impatiently.

"It's really not," I inform her. "If I tie my shoes wrong I don't risk smothering someone to death."

"If I can't breathe, *I'll tell you*." She rolls her eyes at me in the mirror. "Come on. You just tighten the two loops on the back and do the bunny ears. I promise I won't let you bruise my ribs."

What would a Dom do? Well, he certainly wouldn't chicken out on this. With a confidence I don't feel, I grab one of the sets of loops and start pulling it tight. Tighter. She's right, it is a little bit like tying shoes, except tying shoes doesn't give me a hard-on. The more I think about how much I really don't want an erection right now, the more determined it becomes.

She takes in a sharp breath. "Okay. That's it. Tie it there."

I do.

The next one is easier, and I'm harder. Thank God she's standing in front of me in the mirror. Her tiny gasp as I cinch the corset tighter sends an almost painful throb to my groin.

"That's a little too much," she tells me, her voice a little breathless. "Let it out."

I stand there, still holding the ribbons, wondering how she'd react if I threw her down on the bed right now.

"Let it out!" she insists, glaring at me. "Dean?"

I grin at her reflection. "What's the magic word?"

"Go fuck yourself." She tries to twist around, but I let the ribbons slack a little and tie them off.

"Asshole," she snaps when I finally let her go. She turns around to face me. "I swear I'm -"

That's when she notices it. She stops mid-sentence, stares, tries to look like she's not staring, deflates slightly, and blushes a deep red.

"Um," she says, sidestepping around me to the doorway. "We're going to be late. I'll meet you in the car."

If she imagines she's doing me a favor by giving me a chance to jerk off in the bathroom, she's absolutely right.

The car ride is silent and awkward. She's slipped out of her coat and shawl since it's toasty-warm in the car, a bit too toasty-warm to be strictly comfortable in leather pants. And it's even less comfortable with her tits calling to me like a homing beacon from the other side of the backseat.

How can I *not* look? They're pushed up high and proud, the corset doing its job like a goddamn professional. I could get lost in that cleavage.

You used to have those in your bed every day, asshole. Didn't appreciate them then, did you?

Fine. Maybe I took her for granted a little bit. Maybe more than a little. But I never saw her like this before. It's not just her clothes, it's the way she holds herself. She looks a little bit regal and a little bit sly, and I realize that my inconvenient arousal might've actually tickled her more than she let on.

"You look nice," I tell her, finally.

Great job. Awesome line. Now she'll melt for sure.

"I know." She glances at me sidelong and smiles. Okay, so now we're joking about my boner. At least that's a step away from the awkward silence.

"You know it's not always a compliment," I point out. "Sometimes it's involuntary."

"Right," she says, shifting in her seat a little. "*Sometimes* it is."

Now I can almost see the top of her stocking. I'm pretty sure it's not just those faux-tights that are made to look like it, I think they're the real deal. And I don't know why that makes me want to groan out loud.

"Yes," she says, following my line of sight. With one finger, she hikes her skirt up just enough to show where the garter attaches. "They're thigh-highs."

"Christ." I let my head fall back on the seat.

"*She never dressed like that when we were together*," Lissy intones, mocking my inner monologue. "Am I right?"

I shoot her a look. "Well, you didn't."

"Well, you never asked." She grins, sliding a little bit closer, just enough so she can reach out and grab the end of one of my laces. She can't bend at the waist much, so this gesture puts her breasts approximately two inches from my face. I freeze as she tugs on the end of the thin leather strip, gently. "Also, *neither did you.*"

God damn. The girl wanted me in leather and lace-up flies, I would have done it in a heartbeat. I had no idea. How was I supposed to know?

"That's not fair," I grumble, trying to squirm away from her before my temporarily-dormant dick realizes what's going on. "I didn't know you liked it. *Every* straight man with eyes wants to see his woman in a corset and thigh-highs."

"Oh boy," she says, taking mercy on me and putting a little more distance between us. "I hope you're not about to trot out that old 'women aren't visual' stereotype. Come hang out in some of the online readers' groups I'm in. You'll be in for a world of wonders, my friend."

"I'm not saying women aren't visual, I'm just saying...I mean, is that a thing? Do all women like lace-up leather pants? Nobody talks about it." Too late, I realize I've stumbled into a trap.

"Exactly." She grins. "You know how much time

women spend talking about what they can wear to please men? Why don't you try tipping the scales a little bit?"

"Fine, tell me all the secrets, then." I fold my arms across my chest. "I'll make sure to add them to the agenda of the next Bro's Meeting."

"Um, off the top of my head? Well-tailored suits. Button fly jeans. Dress shirts with the sleeves rolled up to the elbows. Sharp uniforms. Boots. *Cowboy* boots. Cowboy *hats*, if you're into that sort of thing."

My eyes widen a little. "Seriously? This is all common knowledge?"

She shrugs. "I mean, pretty much. Opinions vary, of course. I once knew a guy who told me that his favorite look on a woman was a bikini and sneakers. There's no accounting for taste."

"A bikini and anything is a good option," I inform her, glancing at her chest again. God damn it.

"Yeah, well." She smiles, without it reaching her eyes. "Not really for me."

"Could be," I point out.

But she just shakes her head.

Lissy

Me in a bikini? Seriously? I'd get laughed off the beach. Oh well, his vote of confidence is charming, I guess. I'm still kicking myself for not coming up with a scathing one-liner when I noticed that he got hard when he was lacing me up, but the whole thing just threw me off. At the tail end of our relationship, the bedroom situation had become so tepid I was pretty sure he just didn't want me anymore - if he ever had. He certainly never treated me like those book boyfriends do. Then again, that's fiction.

But when I realized I actually still had the power to turn him on, I was caught in some weird mixture of embarrassment, awe, and the desire to grab it and kiss him.

So, you see my dilemma.

Walking into the ballroom, I'm hit with the distinct, smoky smell of leather. I'm arm-in-arm with Dean, glancing around the room for a familiar face. It doesn't take me long to spot Adrian Risinger and Meg, and it's immediately obvious from their body language that the wager is long over.

Smiling to myself, I disconnect from Dean and wander towards the buffet table. Meg spots me on the way, and waves me over.

"Lana! I didn't know you were going to be here." She's absolutely radiant in an outfit that I can only describe as a classy version of 'sexy secretary.' "How are you?"

"Oh, you know," I reply, because I can't bring myself to say anything else. "So, who won?"

Meg grins. "In the interest of maintaining the peace, we've agreed to call it a draw."

"So *you* did, then." I raise my glass. "Congratulations."

"Thank you." She sips her champagne. "It was damn close, though."

Adrian appears out of nowhere. He's going for a more subtle look with a charcoal-black suit and leather driving gloves. "Stop talking about our sex life," he says. "Hi, Lana."

"Never!" Meg declares, hooking her arm with his.

"It's too thrilling to keep private. Isn't that the whole point of your books?"

"Excuse me," says Adrian, smiling in my general direction. "I need to go have a discussion with my secretary."

"I'm not your - *oh*." He tugs her by the arm as he heads for one of the doors, and she turns to wave at me, eyes sparkling. "Nice to see you again, Lana."

Dean keeps reappearing and disappearing, getting pulled into conversations with pretty much every woman who crosses his path. It takes us forty-five minutes to get to a table and sit down with a few bites to eat, because I feel like I can't leave him alone with them. I mean, who *knows* what could happen?

"You really think I could wear a bikini?" I blurt out.

He stares at me like a deer caught in the headlights. "Of course," he says. "Is this about the salad thing? Because I only meant -"

"Relax. I'm just..." I rotate the stem of my champagne glass. "I'm starting to wonder if I should stop waiting to magically get confident someday, and just go ahead and start faking it until I make it."

"Definitely fake it," says Dean. "You've had plenty of practice."

I roll my eyes. "You realize you just burned *yourself*, right?"

"I do," he says. "Confident people can afford to do that, because we act like everything was intentional. That's all you have to do. It's just like being onstage. When you flub a line, just keep going. Nobody notices, nobody remembers."

He might have a point, but I can't be like him. And I have to keep reminding myself that I'm taking advice from a cheater.

When Dean excuses himself, I immediately pull out my phone and open the texting app. I can't help myself.

I'm bored.

M: That doesn't look like a picture of panties to me.

I'm in public. At a party. I'm just bored, that's all. Feel free to ignore me.

M: You're not bored, you're annoyed. Go on, crawl up on my lap and tell Daddy all about it.

You're a fucking creep.

M: And yet here we are.

Damien told me I'd look good in a bikini.

M: Oh my God, I'm so sorry.

Seriously. I'm not bikini material. It's like he doesn't get it. Why do men never understand why we're insecure? Why do they always take it personally when we don't dress sexy "for them?" It's got nothing to do with them.

M: Darling, men are stupid. We think everything is about us.

I get that, but what's the solution?

M: Put on a damn bikini.

I roll my eyes.

So he doesn't have to compromise? It's all about me just getting over myself?

M: What are you wearing?

There's a slight pause.

M: I'm not trying to start anything. You must be wearing something that sparked this conversation, right?

Corset. Skirt. Thigh-highs.

M: I bet you look delectable.

No matter how sarcastic and obnoxious, he never fails to make me smile.

Obviously, I do. But I can't dress like this all the time.

M: But you could do it more often. For him. For yourself. Didn't I see you post that "how to get a bikini body: step one, get a bikini, step two, put it on your body" thing? Don't talk the talk if you're not going to walk the walk.

It's not that easy.

M: Nothing is ever easy. You wanted a solution, there it is. That's the wonderful thing about relationships: your actual personality might be a crooked Jenga pile of neuroses and dysfunction, but you don't get to act that way anymore. You don't get to keep living your own life. If you try to self-destruct, it'll take both of you down. So put on a fucking bikini and give him a thrill. When he wants to leave the lights on during sex, don't hide. It's a fucking compliment. Act like it.

You should do a blog post about that.

M: I plan on it. Another thing: if you do get that bikini, I want a picture.

Never in a million years, Sir.

M: The next time you want my advice, I'm going to remember that.

"Important correspondence?"

I almost jump out of my skin. Dean's standing behind me. I just pray he didn't notice anything on my screen, because I really do not need that in my life right now. Trying to act casual, I lock my screen and tuck my phone away. "Just checking the time," I tell him, as he walks around and takes the chair across from me. "Did you get lost in there?"

"Got caught up in a conversation," he says, glancing at the corner of the room he must've just emerged from. "I didn't expect to be *this* popular."

"It's the pants," I tell him. "Has to be the pants. I mean, it's obviously not your personality."

"That lady over there thought I was *very* charming, I'll have you know," he informs me, jerking his head in the direction of a middle-aged woman in a black dress and studded collar, talking animatedly to someone who looks like she wants badly to escape the conversation.

"I'm sure she did. She looks like she's about five martinis deep. She would find a Cenobite charming."

Dean chuckles. "See, now, I get that reference. I bet you never thought I'd be into horror movies, did you?"

"I admit I didn't." It was one of those points of conflict in our relationship - one that you never talk about, because there's no reason to, but I ended up missing almost everything I wanted to see in theaters and began to resent him for it, without ever mentioning why.

"This is fun, though," Dean says. "Is there anything else coming up soon?"

"Nothing that calls for leather pants," I tell him with a sympathetic smile.

He shakes his head. "Damn it."

CHAPTER EIGHT

For You

I'm still a little tipsy when the car service drops us off at my apartment. Thankfully, Dean is there to help me up the stairs in my damn heels.

"You look beautiful tonight," he says, glancing at me. A smile plays at his lips. "Maybe I should stay in a hotel."

"What does that mean?" I'm fumbling with my keys, and it's not because of the champagne in my system.

"I don't know if I can be trusted." His hand rests on the small of my back. "It was fun, pretending you belonged to me."

"Who says *I'm* the submissive?" I grin at him as I push the door open. For some reason, I'm not shrugging off his hand, but when I start walking forward, he lets me go.

"Everything about you says you're the submissive," he tells me. "That's a compliment, by the way."

"Thank you?" I toss my coat on the sofa and pull off my shoes. "Ugh. Finally."

"Shame," he says, eyes glittering as he looks at me. "But you shouldn't keep torturing yourself on my account."

"Please don't say 'that's my job.'" I meet his eyes, carefully, trying to figure out if he's being even slightly serious.

"I wasn't going to," he says, taking a step closer. "Unless of course..."

I laugh nervously. "What's gotten into you?"

And that's it. The mood changes. With a sudden shrug, Dean flops down on the sofa. "Nothing. Just messing around. Tonight was fun; I thought I'd try and extend it a little bit."

"Yeah," I admit, sitting down an appropriate distance from him. "I guess it's been a while since we had fun together, huh?"

"A very long time." His hands are resting in his lap and I can't stop staring at his fingers, the way they interlock. I miss the feeling of them brushing against my skin, even just casually.

I don't really want to talk about this, but I have a feeling it's going to happen anyway.

"You know," he says, "I had tickets for *Les Mis* the week after we broke up. I was going to surprise you."

I swallow, hard. "No, you never mentioned that."

"You changed, that day," he says, slowly. "I never would've guessed you were capable of hating me."

I stare at him, my throat tightening. "I didn't hate

you."

It's not until now, this exact moment, that I realize how true it is. In the moment I first understood his betrayal, I split in two. A part of me had to hate him, just to survive. It was the mask I showed him that day when he came home, but I didn't realize it at the time. For months afterwards, I constantly wavered between the two identities, one cold and detached, the other wounded. Reeling. And still very much in love.

I thought the wounded half had died, but now I realize she is still very much alive. Mewling for attention, begging for the man she loves, incapable of understanding that he's the one who hurt her.

I don't have the energy to hate him anymore. If anything, I hate *her*.

She's the one who leans forward and touches his arm, who closes the distance between us. She's the one who only sees a man that she still wants, still needs, and kisses him.

There is a moment where he registers surprise, and I think he might actually pull away. But he doesn't.

Dean

She kisses me.

I don't know what it was, but something I did, something I said, melted the ice around her heart. She's willing to forget for a minute that she wishes me dead, and just *feel*.

I should put a stop to it. This is a really, really bad idea. Things are messy and complicated enough as it is.

But she makes this little sound, a muffled whimper, and it brings something roaring to life inside of me.

Fuck yeah, I can give her what she wants. I may not be a book boyfriend, but I know what makes her hot. My hand slides around the back of her neck, holding her head in place, firmly. Taking control of the kiss. My mouth devouring hers. She goes rigid for a second, and then suddenly becomes pliant.

Oh, yes. There's my girl.

My mind is racing and bouncing all over the place, thinking back to all the times we were in bed together, and it seemed like she'd freeze up. The memories are fragmented, but they come back. Every time, I'm almost positive, it's because I was asking her what she liked, what she wanted. Softly and kindly and sweetly, the way you're supposed to do with someone you care about. I remember the intense feeling of frustration when she'd just blush and shake her head, her favorite answer always a murmured: "I dunno."

Now, I get it. She's not embarrassed about sex, she's just a submissive, through and through. She didn't know how to ask to be dominated. I mean, it's a hell of a contradiction. I can't really blame her, although a little part of me wonders how different things could have been between us.

My heart beats wildly in my chest, and needless to say, my dick could probably cut glass. I'm thinking of all the possibilities. Everything she probably wanted me to do, all the desires hidden behind that bashful *I dunno*.

I can be that man. I know my way around her body, where to kiss and touch, although I'll be the first to admit I stopped putting the knowledge to good use at some point. I got complacent, I guess. We both withdrew into ourselves. I'm still selfish, but now I realize that doesn't have to be a bad thing. I very *selfishly* want to see her fall to pieces. I know I can do it. I want to prove I'm not still the guy who fell into the habit of seven minutes of missionary every two weeks, only to roll over and fall asleep. I don't think I could be that guy again.

Because, you know, there's sex, and then there's *sex*. Most men don't struggle to get theirs, so the journey of erotic exploration is mostly left to the frustrated and unsatisfied women who'd like to *really enjoy themselves, just this once*. It's a stereotype, I guess, but it's true. Men are wired to ejaculate. The species can't continue if we don't. As long as that happens, nothing else really matters to our lizard brains. And so millions of years of evolution have left us with a generation of two-pump chumps who may or may not even *enjoy* the sex they're having, but hey, at least they're fulfilling their biological imperative.

We have no motivation to push back against it, unless, of course, we suddenly discover what it means to *really* be turned on.

This isn't about scratching an itch, relieving pressure so I can go to sleep. There's a roaring sensation in my head that's begging me to bend her over the sofa and leave bite marks in the soft flesh of her ass. To spank her until the wetness of her arousal trickles down her leg. To lick it up, taste it, to lose myself in her pleasure. None of those things make any kind of sense biologically. And yet I have this primal need to make her scream.

I pull away from her, finally, trying to catch my breath. I know I won't be able to. Not until I've satisfied the needs writhing and twisting inside me.

"Get up," I tell her roughly.

This is the moment when she might stop, might back away. Might run. But somehow I know she won't.

She stands, unsteadily, swallowing hard. Her eyes are closed.

"Turn around," I whisper.

She does. She's now standing in front of me, body quivering, waiting.

"Take off your skirt."

She unfastens it, and it falls easily to the side. My breath catches in my throat at the sight of the black lace panties, stark on her skin, showing much more than they conceal. I run my finger along the intricate design, watching goose bumps rise along her skin as she feels the warmth of my touch through the flimsy fabric.

Finally, my finger hooks on the waistband, pulls it slightly, and lets it snap back. She gasps.

"Who are these for?" I murmur.

I hear her swallow again, and then she answers. "None of your business."

I stand up, and she spins around to stare at me with wide, dark eyes.

"Bend over the sofa," I tell her.

Her pulse pounds visibly in her throat. "Why?"

I let a humorless smile twist my mouth. "You know why."

A silent battle is waged between us. She has the option to walk away, probably *should* walk away, and she knows it. Oh, but she wants my punishment. She wants me. She hates it, but she's about to forget everything but the feel of my hand.

"You don't have the right," she whispers. "Why

should I?"

"Because you want it so bad you don't care *who* gives it to you," I tell her. "Bad girls can't be choosers."

She laughs, low and throaty. "You think it would be hard to find a guy on Craigslist to spank me, if that's what I really wanted?"

"So get the fuck out, then," I tell her, calmly. The tone is probably somewhat belied by my ridiculous hard-on, but there's nothing to be done about that.

She just glares at me.

"That's what I thought." I smirk. "Bend over and take your punishment."

And she does. I don't know how many guys she's done this with since we were together, but she sure knows how to assume the position like a champ.

"Let's try again." I tug lightly on the panties. "Who are these for?"

"None of your business," she repeats.

I draw my hand back, and I spank her.

The involuntary noise that escapes from her throat just makes me throb harder. It's part pain, part shock, and all arousal. Without even realizing it, she arches her back as much as the corset allows, really displaying her ass to me like the gift that it is. I reach up and fumble with the ribbons, loosening it just enough to really let her express herself.

"Who are these for?"

"Nobody."

Smack.

"Who are these for?"

"It doesn't matter."

Smack.

"Who are these for?"

"Me."

Smack.

"Who are these for?"

"Fuck you."

Smack.

"Maybe, if you're lucky. Who are these for?"

She falls silent. I pick up my pace. One, two, three, four, five, in quick succession, each one harder than the last.

She whimpers.

"Who are these for?" I lay my palm flat on her ass, grabbing a handful of quickly reddening flesh. "You better get it right."

"You," she whispers, at last.

I didn't know that was the answer I was looking for. But it tells me what I need to know. She's surrendering to me, at least for tonight. At least for now.

I grab a fistful of her hair and pull her upright. My body's pressed tight against hers, cock aching to be let free, but I don't. Not yet.

Lissy

"Tell me now if you don't want this." His voice rasps in my ear, and it's a useless thing to say because he knows I can't. I'm incapable. I moan softly as his fingers finally slip underneath the waistband of my panties, sliding down and dipping in just enough to feel how hot and wet I am.

I'm beyond turned on, and he knows it. I both hear and feel the sharp intake of breath as he explores my swollen lips, fingers finally stroking along either side of the hard bud at the apex. I cry out softly, knees buckling.

I wonder if he's thinking about the fact that I was never like this before. Not for him. He's never felt me this needy, never experienced my body turned up to such a fever pitch.

"You want to come?" he asks, softly, almost sing-songy like this is some kind of fucking game. It's not about what I want anymore. I'm aching, deep in my pelvis - is *this* what it feels like when girls get blue balls?

"Fuck you," I grit out, and he chuckles.

His fingers press harder against my most sensitive spot, and I gasp, pressing my ass against him, feeling his cock twitch heavily in response. He ruts against me for a moment, seeming to lose himself, before he remembers that he's supposed to be teasing me.

"All right, then," he pants, and I begin to realize he's almost in the same state I am. Fuck if that doesn't take me a notch higher, my blood pulsing in my veins, head swimming. "Come for me."

He rubs slowly but firmly, in little circles. Normally I need more. More speed, more rhythm, just more. But this isn't normal. I clench deep inside, and he starts moving against me, really thrusting in earnest this time, as the sparks go off behind my closed eyelids and I shout wordlessly, supported only by his arm around my waist, holding me up.

I come for so long I forget my own name.

His hips stutter against me and I start to regain my awareness of reality. I know what those sharp breaths in my ear mean.

"Dean," I whisper, intending to tell him to wait just

a second, because he just gave me the best orgasm of my life and he deserves better than dry-humping. I want him inside me.

But he just groans incoherently, and I know I'm too late. Even through the leather I can feel him pulsing and swelling as he spills his come, and yeah, it's a little bit intoxicating that I turned him on as much as he turned me on. So much he couldn't wait, couldn't even undress enough to jerk off onto me. All he could do was rut against me like we're wild animals, desperation taking over and ruining all semblance of good sense.

It's more than a little intoxicating.

"I was going to tell you to fuck me," I gasp, still out of breath somehow.

"Sorry," he mutters. "I'll get back to you about that in about twenty minutes." He seems to contemplate this for a moment. "...ten?"

Giggling softly, I try to take a step forward on shaky legs.

"Don't." His lips are pressed against the back of my neck. "Where are you going?"

"To bed," I purr. "Unless you were just bluffing."

He lifts his fingers to my lips and I part for him, licking them eagerly, tasting myself. "You want me that bad, huh?" he murmurs. "Can't get enough."

I nod, mouth still full of his fingers.

"Can't hear you," he growls, pulling them away abruptly.

"Yes, Sir," I tell him, breathlessly, accidentally slipping into the same exact phrasing I'm supposed to use with M. Not that it's uncommon. But still, it feels strange.

When we stumble through the doorway and fall

into my bed, I can't stop giggling. I don't know why. There's nothing particularly funny about this, and it's especially not going to be funny in the morning when I really have a chance to reflect on what I've done.

"What?" Dean is grinning as he grabs my wrists, pinning me down on the mattress.

"That was the best sex we've ever had, and we didn't even have sex." I lick my lips, trying to remember how he tastes.

"Not yet," he murmurs, leaning in and planting a series of feather-light kisses on my face and neck. "Just wait until you find out what else I've learned how to do."

CHAPTER NINE

The Storm

Lissy

My family, of course, wants to go "clothes shopping in the city." After living here for as long as I have, I'm no longer enamored of the many boutiques and stores that send tourists into a frenzy. And not just because it's so hard to find anything that fits me there.

Thankfully, my family's respective budgets keep us from spending too long in the places where the clerks seem like they're staring through your soul if you're over a size two. We're at a place that's more my speed now, and I might actually pick up a few things. I could probably use some pajamas that don't have holes in them.

It's February, which naturally means that the

swimsuits are out. I find myself looking for a little too long at the bikinis.

I mean, maybe M's right. Maybe it really can be as simple as making a decision, squeezing myself into a swimsuit, and daring the world to judge me.

Dean and I haven't discussed what happened last night. He was already awake when I got up, so I'm not even sure if he spent the night in my bed.

Whatever. It's not worth thinking about. It's not like it...*meant* something, or anything like that.

My hand drifts across a rack and stops on something strappy with a pretty nice green pattern.

"Really?" Dean grins at me. "I thought for sure that was just the champagne talking when you started asking me about bikinis again."

"Yeah, well." I pick up the bottoms and stretch them out to full size, cringing a little. Is that really what I look like? "I've been thinking about it."

"Thinking," he repeats. He's skeptical and I don't know why, but it bugs me.

"I talked to a friend," I admit, finally, to get him off my back. He doesn't need to know who the "friend" is. "I realized maybe I've been unfair to myself."

And unfair to you.

I didn't want to think about it at the time, but all that stuff about turning off the lights during sex and shooting down ideas of sexy outfits - yeah, that was me. I didn't realize how I was probably chipping away at Dean's ego in little bits and pieces, every time I unknowingly demonstrated that I didn't really care how sexy he thought I was. My own insecurities mattered more.

Nothing excuses what he did, but if I could go

back and do it over? I'd be different. I would, in the immortal words of M, wear a damn bikini.

It's too late now, of course. Sure, we had sex last night - a few times - but I'm not getting entangled with him again. Now that I know what kind of person he is, I'd be insane to let him get under my skin. But there's no harm in a little no-strings-attached fun.

I can picture Jack giving me a very disapproving look. I brush it away.

In the end, I find myself in a fitting room with a couple "fatkinis" slung over my arm. That's what they call them on the fashion blogs, I think. The high-waisted numbers that still show a lot more skin than I'm comfortable with. I have a feeling this is going to end badly, but I try one on anyway.

"Nope!" I say, out loud.

"Everything okay in there?" my mom calls out.

"Yep," I shout back, turning away from the mirror. "Never been better."

Because my life has spun completely out of control, I text M from the fitting room of the next store my sisters drag me into.

Just for the record, I tried a bikini. It was a disaster. 0/10, would not recommend.

M: Let me be the judge of that.

I didn't take a picture. Trust me. I looked like Shamu.

M: That's not very attractive, you know.

I'm aware.

M: No. I mean the way you talk about yourself. If you act like you're sexy, everyone will believe it.

I don't think it really works that way. I live in New York City. There are actual beautiful people here.

M: I've been to New York, you know. I'm not a farmer.

I guess I've never thought about where you live before.

M: Don't get derailed, Lana.

So are you near here?

M: I come there for business often enough. It's not too far.

I don't know why that makes my heart leap in my chest. We're never going to meet. Ever.

Huh.

M: Huh. Why the sudden interest?

I've just always been curious.

M: Really.

Really.

M: I don't believe you.

Believe it. I'm not angling for anything.

M: Do you know this hotel?

The next message is a link to one of the nicer places downtown. I think I've probably gone past it a few times, although I've never stayed there. Never had any reason to.

More or less.

M: If you ever decide you want to see me, go there. Book a room. I know you can afford it. Text me your room number and I'll be there.

I actually snort out loud. How ridiculous of a proposition is that? Does he think he's the mysterious billionaire from one of these books? Nobody acts like that in real life.

Haha, okay.

M: Did I say something funny?

You really expect me to do that?

M: Sweetheart, I know you will.

You're insane.

M: And you're being awfully disrespectful.

What are you going to do, come over here and punish me?

M: Won't be long until you're begging me for it. But no. I know you're not ready to meet me.

It's not a question of being ready, I'm not interested.

M: Don't want to make this too real, hm?

That's not why.

M: Afraid someone will find out?

No. I just don't want to. This is fun, but I have no interest in escalating.

M: I beg to differ. Everything that's happened between us is pure escalation. It's only a matter of time.

Well, you keep that hope alive.

M: Have you ever been spanked?

My face starts burning. There's no way I'm ready to admit that happened between me and Dean, even without the shameful backstory and the tiny fact that we happen to be broken up.

Not the way you're talking about.

M: You write about it an awful lot for someone who's never experienced it.

"A lot?" Two books. I write to the market.

M: Right. So you only write about spanking because of Fifty Shades.

Yep.

M: I don't like it when you lie to me.

Why do you care if I'm curious? You can't do it. You'll never get to even touch my ass, let alone smack it.

M: When I've got my cock buried inside you someday, I'm going to remind you that you said that.

I close the app quickly, my heart pounding.

"Um, Lissy?"

I walk towards my bedroom doorway where Dean is standing, staring up.

"Yes?" I say, slowly.

"There seems to be a tiny problem with your..." He steps back. "...ceiling. Situation."

By "problem," he means a giant, sagging leak, nearly the size of my bed.

Because, of *course*.

We just managed to extricate ourselves from the

all-day grasp of my parents, and now my goddamn ceiling is caving in. I don't even have the energy to be upset about it.

I pull out my phone and call emergency maintenance, where the receptionist is the only person in the world who sounds calmer about a massive ceiling leak than I do.

"Must be all the snow," I comment, in hopes of some human interaction with her, but all I get the sound of tap-tapping on the keyboard.

Finally, I hang up in disgust.

"They'll have somebody over to staple up some plastic," I mutter, tossing my phone on the sofa. "I could've done that myself. They won't be able to do the proper repairs until tomorrow."

"Guess you'll be joining me in the living room," he says. "You can have the sofa."

"Well, we can get hotel rooms," I muse, remarkably calm considering there's probably about to be fucking hole in my *fucking ceiling*.

"Uh, you're kidding, right?" Dean's looking at me like I just suggested building a homestead on Pluto for the night.

"Why would I be kidding? I know it's a bad storm, but there has to be..." I glance at the window, like that's going to tell me anything.

"It's also *Fashion Week*," Dean cuts in.

"Fuck." I stare at him. "Seriously? How do you know this stuff?"

"Well, I try to make it a habit to have some situational awareness," he deadpans. "Besides, we do some of their marketing at my firm. The dates are permanently burned into my retinas."

So that's how we end up splitting a bottle of wine on the living room floor, with cheese and crackers and laughing about how insanely overbearing my family has become. I love them, I love them to death, but if I make it to the end of next week without killing anyone, it'll be a miracle.

Halfway through our second poker game, he nudges his foot against mine. "Why the long face? I can't imagine you've got anything to be worried about."

"No, my life's going exactly as expected. Are you kidding? I'm sitting on my living room floor, trying to ignore that sound that might be wind whistling through a giant hole in my bedroom ceiling, playing cards with my ex." I smile ruefully. "What else could I possibly want in life?"

"Marketing *is* lying," I insist. "Lying by omission at best, but it's still a lie."

I have no idea why or how we started arguing, but I'm fully committed to it now. These are, apparently, the kinds of things that happen when you think you just heard the sound of wet drywall falling in your bedroom, and you're afraid to go assess the damage.

He snorts. "I guess if you think it's 'lying' when you go on a first date and don't tell somebody all the worst things about you immediately. Nobody expects ads to be honest. It's about putting your best foot forward."

I roll my eyes at him, leaning back and stretching my legs in front of me. "So you don't think it's lying if all the models in shampoo ads are wearing extensions? And the dogs in all those shitty kibble ads are really eating organic raw-food diets prepared by world-class veterinary nutritionists, to make their coats all glossy for TV? I'm not talking about presentation, or putting your best foot forward. They're showing you 'results' that have nothing to do with the products they're pushing, and they're allowed to do it - as long as they put a tiny disclaimer in the corner that nobody reads."

"Everybody knows that ads aren't real," he insists. "I might as well say that your books are irresponsible, because they give people unrealistic expectations about love."

"That's not the same thing!" I shake my head at him. "I'm not saying 'buy this book and you'll have this kind of relationship in your real life.' I'm just saying 'buy this book and enjoy the fantasy.' There's nothing deceptive about that."

"There's nothing deceptive about hair extensions," Dean replies. "No one actually thinks their hair is going to look like that if they buy the shampoo."

"Of course they do. Maybe not consciously, but..."

"Please tell me you're not going to get into subliminal advertising." Dean holds up his hand. "Because if you do, this conversation is *over*."

"I'm not talking about subliminal, I'm talking about subconscious. It's like what you were saying at lunch the other day. Our brains draw a connection between the model's amazing hair and the shampoo she's talking about, without any conscious thought on our parts. It's just how it *works*. The whole point of advertising is to hack into that connection and use it to sell stuff. Bottles full of chemicals that are probably actively damaging your hair, but hey, Tina Fey's wig sure looked luxurious on TV!" I let out a sharp sigh, hating the argumentative version of me that always rears its head when Dean is involved.

"That's just the business." Dean leans back, stretching his legs out in front of him. "If my guys don't hire the production company that provides the stylist that clips in Tina's fake hair, then somebody else is going to."

"You could use the same logic to just throw all your garbage on the street, because hey, there's going to be litter no matter what *you* do."

He shakes his head. "That was always your problem, Lissy. Nobody can live their lives with one hundred percent integrity. It doesn't work that way. It's just not possible. We're all hypocrites, in one way or another. We all lie, we all hide things, we all obscure the truth. If you keep going around expecting people to act like Captain America, you're going to be disappointed for the rest of your life."

"This isn't about you and me," I mutter, staring at my lap. "But of course you'd think that."

"I promise you I'm right," he says. "There's no such thing as integrity, only the people who've done a really great job of hiding their lies."

"Liars always say that." I glare at him. "Did you ever even love me, or was that just *business*, too?"

Oh boy. Where did *that* come from? I stare at the empty wine bottle next to me.

Damn it, this is your fault.

"Lissy." He squeezes his eyes shut. "Don't do this."

It's a valid question, it's just that I sound like a crazy person bringing it up out of the blue in the middle of a fight. And worse than that, I sound like I'm not over him.

"You seem to think the answer is obvious." I grab

another bottle of wine and wrench it open while Dean looks on, wincing slightly at my clumsiness. "It's not. It never was. What happened the other night..." Damn it, now there's a lump in my throat. This isn't how this is supposed to go. "...that was the first time I felt like you really wanted me."

Then, he says something I don't expect.

"I know," he says. "It was different." He shakes his head slowly. "Of course it wasn't the first time I wanted you. You were beautiful when I met you."

He sounds remarkably calm, considering how I just snapped on him like an overstretched rubber band. I don't know what to say, so I just let him keep going.

"But you're even more beautiful now," he says, his eyes locking with mine. "It's killing me, Lissy."

We almost knock over the wine bottle when our bodies crash together, sprawling out on the floor. He kisses me like he wants to devour every part of me, his hands roaming across my body, sliding under my camisole until his fingers sink into the soft flesh of my breasts, stiffened nipples rasping against his palms.

Everything inside me sparks to life. I clutch at his back, feeling the muscles tense and tighten under my fingers. I'm breathless when he finally breaks away.

"Beg me to taste you," he whispers, eyes burning into mine.

My nails dig deeper into his back, and he winces. I'm calling his bluff.

"No."

He snarls. "Goddamn it, Lissy." Rearing up, he grabs my pajama pants and yanks them down. I squirm under his heated gaze, but I can't bring myself to try and stop him when he plants his hands on my thighs and jerks them apart.

I whine softly as his teeth scrape lightly against sensitive flesh, and I realize he's using them to yank my panties aside, just enough to lick me. And -

My hips buck helplessly, my back arching as I let out a string of curses that I wasn't even aware I knew.

Yes, it's safe to say his technique has improved.

Or maybe it's M's influence that has me wound up into some kind of frenzy. I don't know, and I certainly don't care. My whole body is jerking like a live wire, and *somebody* is making noises, and I'm pretty sure it's me.

God. He's perfect.

The first few ripples of pleasure in my chest aren't a surprise, but then they're building, and, oh -

He stops.

Propping himself up on his elbows, he stares at me, while I do the same, a little more shakily, and stare at him.

"Beg," he growls.

It takes every ounce of my willpower to shake my head.

Dean ducks down for another taste.

"*Unnh.*" My head falls back, chest heaving.

He's staring at me again. I can tell. With a massive effort, I lift my head.

He licks his lips.

"You know what you have to do." His voice is low and rough.

I'm not going to cave.

Oh...

I'm not.

Ffffuuuuuck.

I'm...

Guh.

...being strong, damn it...

Oohh, no. Oh - YES.

Oh, NO.

"You can't," I gasp, pushing myself up again as Dean fixes me with an evil grin.

"I can," he says.

"I'm..."

"I know," he says, softly, his eyes drifting down between my legs. "I'll let you finish, all you have to do is ask."

The absolute bastard. He stopped just as I began to tip over the edge, and I could practically cry from frustration. He knows exactly what he's doing.

Lowering himself back down, slowly, he presses a kiss on the inside of one thigh. And then the other.

I groan softly, my body betraying me and tilting towards his mouth.

He blows a very well-aimed puff of air, and I gasp, then groan his name.

"Please," I whisper, and he chuckles, low and dark.

"I can't hear you."

"PLEASE." I could scream. "Please, Dean, I need..."

Yes. *That.*

Exactly...that.

It's insanely explosive, it's too much, it's not enough. It's everything. It goes on forever, and then my whole body throbs and aches as I come back to my senses.

He kisses me softly, and I taste myself on his mouth.

"Dean..."

His fingers ghost across my lips, silencing me.

"Don't." One single word, murmured against my ear, but I get it.

Don't talk about it. Don't ruin this. For once, let's just be.

And we are. Here. Together. In spite of everything, a strange sense of calm washes over me, so unlike anything I've felt with him before.

I'd always had that sense of rightness with him, even when things were less than perfect. And of course, they always were. After he betrayed me, I thought it was all a lie, just my brain and my hormones playing tricks on me, but now I'm starting to wonder.

Maybe it was all the tension, the drifting apart, the pain and anger and suspicion - maybe *that* was the lie. Maybe we really were meant to be together.

Except we fucked it up. *He* fucked it up. Or maybe it was me. I'm not sure anymore, and it's driving me insane. I don't want to believe that I was wrong about him and Jessica, except I need to. Because there aren't many explanations for his behavior that allow for him to be a decent person.

If he truly did lie to protect my feelings, if his relationship with her was strictly platonic, then I can forgive him. Hell, I've probably done stupider things in my lifetime. But if he hid her existence for any other reason, I just can't wrap my head around it. If he did it knowing, even just in some small, back corner of his mind, that he had feelings for her - committing to me instead was unforgivable. Maybe not in the grand scheme of things. Maybe it's not the kind of thing that sends you to the deepest circle of hell. But for me, in my life? I can't be somebody's second choice.

Even if there was some insurmountable reason why he thought they couldn't be together. Even if he never intended to act on it. Even if he chose me because he couldn't choose her.

After he left, I did a lot of reading up on emotional infidelity. I'd always felt uneasy about the fact that I had no proof of a physical relationship, which put me in some odd outcast category of betrayed spouses. I did try hanging out in a few forums and chatting with some fellow Betrayeds, as they called themselves, but many of them seemed to spend a lot of time warning me that I'd eventually find out that he fucked her. (They used gentler terminology, but the sentiment was there.) It was like they were trying to help me ward off the Demon of Eventual Truth. I explained to them that we weren't really talking anymore, that I had never even met her, that there was no way I'd accidentally stumble across the information - but they warned me all the same. People don't leave for purely emotional affairs, they'd tell me. The fact that he walked away was basically an admission of guilt.

It's been two years, and still not a shred of evidence. When I called him up to see if he'd help me with my little problem, I half expected him to say he couldn't. I had no particular reason to believe he was single, but he was. No Jessica in sight. Not that infidelity-based relationships tend to last very long, but I would've thought there'd be *somebody*.

This is going to drive me insane. I have to know.

CHAPTER TEN

What Happened

Two Years Ago

Dean and I don't keep any secrets from each other. There's no need to. We're perfectly in sync, and our relationship has become effortless.

People always talk about relationships being "hard work," but it hasn't been that way for us in a long time. We've grown used to each other's quirks, adjusted to our respective roles in the relationship, and I'm wonderfully content.

"You know what I've been craving lately?" I ask him as we sit side-by-side on the train.

He shakes his head.

"Drunken noodles, from that Thai place. You want

to go tonight?"

He shakes his head regretfully. "I can't, Lissy. Gotta work late."

"Again? Seriously?" I sigh, leaning back in the seat. These days, it seems like it's always crunch time. I want to ask him why he can't just skip one of his lunchtime runs and get out early instead, but there's no denying he looks damn good these days from all the exercise. So good, in fact, I'm starting to wonder just how much those "quick" runs are starting to encroach on his workday.

"I'm sorry," he says. "I promise I won't be jealous if you go. Just make sure to bring me some home."

"Ugh. Eating out alone is the saddest feeling in the world." I lean my head on his shoulder. "Maybe tomorrow night?" I suggest hopefully.

"Maybe," he says. "I'll have to see how much progress I make."

I get off a few blocks before he does, and we share quick kiss goodbye. I've got applications to drop off at a few temp agencies, and I need to check my P.O. box to see if any of the magazines I've submitted to have bothered to reject me yet.

I waste as much time as I can, ingratiating myself to office staff and sorting through my junk mail. After heading back home, I give serious thought to cleaning out the fridge while refreshing my email, waiting to hear back from someone. Anyone. A zine, an anthology, a job offer - anything. We can live pretty comfortably on Dean's salary at the marketing firm, but I hate feeling useless.

As dinnertime rolls around, I find I can't stop thinking about those drunken noodles. I don't know exactly how they make them, but it's such a delicious, savory-sweet, spicy dish full of fresh veggies and homemade noodles. Completely addictive, and I know I won't stop obsessing until I can get some. The place doesn't normally do takeout, but I have a feeling I'll be able to convince them to make an exception just once.

Romantic gestures aren't really my thing. Dean and I have never needed that kind of stuff. I don't want expensive jewelry - I'd lose it - or flowers that will just wilt and die. And Dean? Well, if he wants anything more from me, he's certainly never said anything about it. But just this once, I think it'd be nice to surprise him. Even if he can't take much of a break from his work, it'll be fun to have a little dinner in companionable silence. I'm not clingy and needy anymore, I've grown up since the early days of our relationship. But when he's working late all the time, I find I do miss him.

It takes me a while, and a lot of head-shaking and apologies from the staff, but I finally manage to get the manager's attention and he says he'll do it for a small extra fee. They've already got the containers for dine-in patrons, so it's just a matter of sweet-talking them into it. Half an hour later, I emerge triumphant with two containers full of the most delectable food imaginable.

My mouth is watering as I sit on the subway, dodging a few jealous looks from hungry commuters. It smells amazing, and it's a good thing they didn't have plastic forks at the restaurant, or I'd be attacking mine now.

I'm hoping to surprise him, but when I arrive at the agency, it looks dark inside. Tugging on the doors reveals that this clandestine mission is going to be a little more difficult than I thought.

I could call him, but instead I try the agency's number, hoping that a receptionist or someone else might be staying late. After a lot of rings, someone finally does pick up.

"Hi, I know you're closed," I tell her, so she doesn't think I'm some nutty client. "This is Felicity Warden, I'm Dean Summer's girlfriend. I know he's working late and I just wanted to stop by with some takeout I picked up. Is there any way you could let me in? I wanted to surprise him."

There's a moment of silence, during which my primary concern remains whether or not I sound like some kind of crazy stalker trying to break into the building.

In the next moment, my world ends.

He left a few hours ago.
He left a few hours ago.
He left a few hours ago.

The words are still ringing in my ears. There has to be an explanation for this. A romantic surprise! If I lived in a movie, I might believe it. But that's not how Dean and I are. That's not how we've ever been.

The receptionist tells me, reluctantly, that he's gone running in the park a few blocks down. I can tell from the look on her face that he's not alone, but I wasn't going to make her tell me anything more.

I just go there myself, prepared to see the worst.

Maybe he *is* alone. Maybe I'm paranoid. Maybe he just decided, last minute, to go on a really long run. Maybe work didn't take as long as he thought, and he just needed to blow off some steam.

I go to the park and I sit on the bench, and I wait.

Joggers are going by, some solo, some clustered in pairs or trios. They're all single-minded, focused on the simple goal of making one more lap. Just one more.

And then, I see him.

Running alongside him, keeping his pace perfectly, is a woman. She's tan and gorgeous and her running clothes look more expensive than my fanciest outfits. I have the sudden urge to run and hide, but I feel rooted to the spot. He gets closer.

She points to something in the pond, and he slows his pace slightly. Laughs. When he looks at her, he does it with a certain intensity, like he really cares what she has to say. Like he's really listening.

When was the last time he looked at me that way?

As they share some private joke, they draw even closer. Pretty soon, he'll see me.

What am I going to say to him?

What am I going to do?

He runs past.

He runs past, looking at the girl beside him, and he doesn't see me.

It's like I don't even exist.

I could scream, I could run after him, but I don't. I just sit there for a moment, frozen in space, my heart pounding so hard I feel like it's shaking my entire body.

I go home, because I don't know what else to do. I think about calling him, telling him to come back here immediately, but I don't. I want to see how long he'll be gone. I need to know, even though every passing minute feels like walking on shards of glass.

I realize I still have the drunken noodles in my hand, and I put them into the fridge, carefully. It's tempting to throw them away, but they deserve more respect than that. No need to get them caught up in this mess.

At one point, I actually manage to eat a few mouthfuls. My stomach is growling in spite of myself, because I don't feel hungry, but I know I need food. My head starts racing, heart leaping with all the possibilities I'd have as a single woman. I could move anywhere! Do anything!

Of course, there's the small issue of having no money. That might be a problem.

Despair sets in again, and then anger, and then a series of emotions that can only be described by Kelly Clarkson songs. By the time I hear Dean's key click in the lock, I've settled into a stage of icy calm that belies how fast my heart is pounding.

He's talking almost before the door opens all the way. "I'll tell you what, if they don't do something about all the construction on the..."

And that's when he sees my face.

"What's wrong, Lissy?" he asks, looking concerned.

"I stopped by your office tonight," I tell him, quietly. I watch as the words sink in, the color draining from his face. "Where were you?"

"I don't know what you mean," he says, his voice very quiet. He's still just standing there, frozen, in the doorway. "I was...maybe I stepped out for a minute? The receptionist is new, she doesn't..."

"Stop it!" I shout, jumping to my feet. "*I saw you at*

the park with her. If you're not about to tell me the truth, the entire truth...then just get the fuck out."

He sighs heavily, coming towards the sofa and sitting down. I hug my arms tighter around my torso and stare at him, waiting.

"It's been too busy to go on my runs during lunch," he says. Slowly, deliberately, like he's measuring every word. "I was plateauing. I had to start working in longer distances somehow, but it just wasn't going to fit in. Not in the middle of the workday. So I started going after."

And here it comes.

"She's my running partner, Lissy," he says, finally. "Her name is Jessica. She's a friend from work. I knew you wouldn't...because of what happened with you and Andrew, I knew you wouldn't be okay with it."

"And that's it?" I demand, jumping to my feet. "A running partner?"

"That's..." he shakes his head. "It's not what you think, Lissy. I swear. I know how this looks."

"I don't think you do." I'm trembling all over, but I won't back down. "I would have been fine with you having a running partner, and you know that. So why lie? Why hide it?"

"It wasn't just that," he says, quietly. "She's a good friend. A close friend. She has been for a long time."

I'm starting to piece it together, even through the lies. I can see it in his face. "Since before me."

He nods, wincing a little. "After you told me about Andrew and what he did to you, I figured..." He exhales heavily. "I figured it was better if you just didn't know she existed. I didn't want you to..."

"Hassle you?" I demanded. "Ask too many

questions you didn't want to answer?"

"Worry!" he almost shouts, standing up and pacing halfway across the room in a single breath. "I knew it would freak you out, okay? I was scared of losing you. But I didn't want to give up the best friendship of my life, either. I thought I could have both. She and I would just spend time together at work, and that would be it. That would be our time."

The idea of him planning out this secret life, his special time with another woman while I sat at home alone - my stomach roils.

He's starting to calm down a little and realize how it sounds, but it's too late to take the words back now. "It's not that I...it's just, she's different. You know? There's a reason why people have friends. It was never like that with us, because she's not *you*. But she always pushed me, and motivated me, and if it weren't for her, I probably would've just quit running." He rakes his hands through his hair. "I know I fucked up. I know. But please don't turn this into something it's not."

"So you expect me to believe," I say, quietly, "that from the very beginning, you've been hiding a friendship you have with another woman...because...I just wouldn't *get* it?"

"I know how it sounds," he says, again. He sounds tired.

"Once again, *I don't think you do*." My mind is reeling. Could he possibly be telling the truth?

No. No. *Fuck* no. I won't let this happen again. I learned my lesson the first time, didn't I? Of all the things I learned with Andrew, there's one that stands out as the most crucial.

Trust your instincts.
Trust your instincts.
Trust your instincts.

When Andrew brought his "friend" around, I ignored the ugly, jealous feeling in the back of my mind. I refused to let my head realize what my heart already knew. I was loving, supportive, and more than that, I trusted him. I trusted him, even when everybody else in the world told me it wasn't normal. That it wasn't right.

She didn't have a lot of money, Andrew's girl. Neither did he, particularly, neither did any of us, but she was still in graduate school. She was always on the verge of some educational or financial disaster, and I remember coaching her through some of them, making her hot chocolate once. Mothering her, almost.

Once she came around, Andrew stopped bothering me about when we were going to start a family. We were both so young, I just wanted to spend a little more time with him, get to know myself, save a little money. I didn't want to raise a baby in a one-bedroom apartment when I had to go down to the street to the laundromat. But this girl, this friend, she suddenly started occupying his time and energy. She was always in need of help or advice.

Andrew's sister took one look at the two of them together, and she told me they were lovers.

I told her she was crazy.

Guess who's crazy now?

After almost a year of this, being gaslighted, being made to feel like a third wheel in my own relationship, I couldn't take any more. I snooped.

You have to understand, that's not me. I'm not that person. But when you feel your life start crumbling out from beneath your feet, you'll find you don't know *what* kind of person you are anymore.

It was all laid out for me, in gory detail. They'd gone out to pick up some dinner together, and I stayed home. Yes, specifically to snoop. Yes, that's who he turned me into.

She had been playing around on his laptop, and when I opened the screen, her accounts were still logged in. Fucking idiot. That stupid, naive little homewrecker. Thinking she was so special. Thinking he wouldn't someday up and leave her, as eagerly as he up and left me.

And that was how it went down. When I confronted them, she ran away crying. I never saw her again. Andrew hurled accusations about what a terrible girlfriend I was, packed a bag, and disappeared.

I told Dean all of this. The whole, devastating story. Now I know the wheels in his head must've been turning that whole time, thinking of his girl, Jessica, the woman on the side. Figuring out how difficult it would be to carry on with her, since I was so suspicious. Deciding how and when and where he would lie.

I don't understand why men do these things. Do they get off on the secrecy? The lies? He could've just had a life with Jessica if he wanted, if they weren't both too cowardly to pursue it. I guess it's easier to keep things casual. No question of going too far or moving too fast if at least one of you stays in another relationship. No moving in together, no dealing with broken dishwashers and sick pets - just sexy, stolen out-of-town weekends. No long-term commitments, only wishes and promises hanging on "wouldn't it be nice."

What's not to like? It's low stakes. You never get

sick of each other, always longing to be together.

It's a honeymoon that never ends.

I guess I do understand it. Dean, unlike Andrew, actually does try a little bit. He keeps trying to convince me that he's telling me the truth. He tells me he'll introduce me to her, and I laugh in his face. As if that would somehow indicate that his penis has never been inside her. As if that's even what matters. Whatever they've done, he feels something for her that he tried to keep a secret from me. That means something. It means more than anything he could tell me in words.

—

CHAPTER ELEVEN

Darts

I've made a resolution not to sleep with Dean again.

It's not going well so far.

"If this is what you wanted, you should've told me," he growls in my ear. I gasp as he yanks my arms behind my back, his hands grasping so tightly around my wrists that it aches.

It started with a conversation in the kitchen. How it ended up in the bedroom is not exactly clear, but I can't argue with the results.

"I didn't think -"

"*You thought wrong.*" His teeth sink into my neck and I moan, shuddering, knees weakening, melting at his touch. It was never like this before. I never knew it *could* be like this. I thought it was all fantasies, in those books - but right now, I feel like I really am Lana.

"Say it," he rumbles in my ear. "Tell me you love being my whore."

I *asked* for this, by the way. That's the effect he has on me.

"I love it," I pant, because...well.

"I'm going to fuck you," he whispers. "Until you scream. Don't try to fake it - I'll know. I want you shattering to pieces. I want your throat so raw you won't recognize your own voice."

What the hell's gotten into him? Who *made* him this way? As conflicted as I feel about it, I kind of want to find the person and kiss them on the mouth.

Or maybe punch them in the stomach. At this point, it's not entirely clear.

By the way - yes. I *do* scream.

More than once.

When he catches me making some special sore-throat tea afterwards, he can't stop smiling.

Dean

I can't believe the mess I've gotten myself into.

Tonight, Lissy's family is split down gender lines. The girls are seeing a Broadway show, and the guys are all trying to kill each other with paintballs. I begged off, saying I had to work late. Yeah, I know. After all the trouble that got me into, you'd think I would've given up the lie. But it works so well.

The Wardens always seem so friendly and accommodating, until you realize they have you in sheer numbers and they'll just steamroll over anyone and anything that doesn't fit their plans. But at least the Warden men appreciate a good solid work ethic, so they only called me "chicken" five or six times. I don't really dislike paintball, but I do dislike the idea of being repeatedly shot in the balls by my fake girlfriend's brothers.

I'm at a bar instead, the kind of dive that tourists don't set foot in. Even if it was close to paintball, there's no risk of running into them here. It's been a favorite of mine for years.

The bartender almost pulls me a lager without asking, but I get a bourbon instead, because I need something that'll hit me hard and fast. Beer takes too long. My thoughts are too sharp, and I need to dull them as quickly as possible.

A guy slides into the stool that's two down from mine, eyes drifting over the taps like he's about to choose from a fancy-ass wine list. I kind of snicker to myself, turning back to my drink.

"Hey, do you have the time?"

I glance up at him, pulling my phone out of my pocket. "Uh, six-fifteen."

"Thanks. I left my phone in a cab." He scowls a little, pulling out his wallet. "Called the company, but..."

"Yeah, you're never getting that back." I manage to suppress another snicker. "Welcome to the Big Apple."

"I actually live here," he says. "First time that's ever happened to me, if you can believe it."

"Wow. Charmed life."

"Tell me about it." He lifts his glass. I didn't pay attention to him ordering, but it's also some kind of brown liquid. Possibly the same one I'm drinking. "Cheers."

"Cheers." I finish the last swallow and set my glass down. "I hope you're not trying to hit on me, because I don't swing that way. No offense."

"In this place?" He grins, looking around him at the sad, abandoned pool table and sticky wood paneling. "No, me neither. Just trying to kill some time in a place that won't blow out my eardrums."

Nodding, I pick up my second drink. "I never really got into the club scene."

"Don't. Trust me." He shakes his head. "Not worth it. The girls are nice, don't get me wrong, and it's fun while it lasts. But eventually you wake up at three P.M. on a Saturday and you realize you're spending almost all of your leisure time rubbing up against sweaty strangers and paying five dollars for a generic bottled water. That's no way to live."

"Could be worse," I chuckle. "At least you're doing *something* other than working."

"I *wish* I was working," he replies ruefully. "What do you do?"

"Marketing." I swallow another mouthful, relishing the burn.

"No shit, Don Draper!" I'm getting a little tired of people calling me that, but I guess it could be worse. He pulls something out of his pocket and rolls it in my direction. "Sell me this pen."

I laugh, grabbing it and shoving it into my own pocket.

"Hey," he says, after a minute. "That's my pen."

"Not anymore," I tell him. "How much will you give me for it?"

He groans. "Okay, I set myself up for that. Good job. I really believe you're in marketing. Give me my pen back."

"Sales and marketing are two different things anyway," I point out, rolling it back to him. "I sell ideas, not pens."

"Same difference," he says. "Either way, it's just about making somebody think you care about their needs."

That one gets a bitter laugh. "Sounds like something my ex-girlfriend would say."

"She doesn't like sales, huh?"

"She always found me to be a little...disingenuous." I shrug. "I mean, in her defense, I guess I'm kind of a liar."

He shrugs. "Aren't we all?"

"Yeah, I guess so." I look down at my drink to realize I've drained it again without even realizing. The guy at the bar hops out of his seat and wanders over to the wall, where a dusty, disused dartboard is hanging precariously from a bent nail.

He grabs a dart and yanks it out of the board, then turns to me. "Want a game? We could bet to make things interesting."

"Loser pays both tabs," I suggest.

"Excellent." He proceeds to pull out the rest of the darts. "As long as you won't stab me in the back."

"I'm a liar, not a backstabber," I insist.

"You know, if you keep saying that, I'm going to insist on knowing what you lied about." He steps a few paces back and stares down the dartboard. "It's obviously something specific. You're feeling guilty. Absolve yourself, my child. I almost thought about becoming a priest once, so I'm well-qualified."

I laugh at him. "How about this. If you win, I'll tell you the story."

"That's fair. But I'll make it more interesting. For every shot I get that's closer to the bulls-eye than yours, I get one question to narrow it down."

He nails the bullseye. Things aren't looking good for me.

I take my shot, and of course it goes wide.

"Okay," he says. "So there's only three things people lie to their girlfriends about. Other women, money problems, and drug problems."

"I don't think that's remotely true," I point out, but he keeps going.

"Tell me which one it was."

I sigh. "Another woman. But not like that."

"Not like that, you say?" He nearly nails the center of the board again. "I didn't say what *that* was, but I'm curious now."

"You're obviously going to win, so, fine." I shrug. "I had this friend. A close friend. She happened to be a woman."

The guy nods, like he understands perfectly.

"Then I met my ex," I go on. "One of the first things she told me about herself was that her last boyfriend totally crushed her, by cheating on her with a 'friend.' Even brought her around the house, basically welcomed her into the family and acted like it was all above-board. Balls of steel. So right away, I knew it was going to be a problem. I didn't want to give up either one of them, so...I lied."

It feels strange to rehash the story, but not necessarily in a bad way. The guy folds his arms across his chest and nods slowly. "And let me guess - when she found out..."

"Right." I sigh. "She assumed the worst, of course, like you would. I mean, who keeps a female friend secret from their girlfriend unless...? But it felt like the only option I had at the time. I knew, even if my ex said she was okay with it at the time, eventually she wouldn't be. There would always be this fear and suspicion. I wanted her to..." I laugh a little bit at myself. "I know this sounds ridiculous, but I wanted her to *trust* me."

"You," the guy says, pointing his finger at me and shaking his head, "need another drink."

I have to agree with him.

CHAPTER TWELVE

A Hill of Beans

Lissy

Yes, I sent Jack on a reconnaissance mission. It's scummy, but I feel pretty scummy these days. I know Jack will get the truth out of him. He always gets to the bottom of things.

It wasn't hard to plan. I know where his favorite dive bar is, and I already know he's got nothing against lying about "working late." I actually didn't expect my first attempt to be successful, but Jack texted me that he'd spotted him, and he was going to work. I hadn't heard anything since, and that was almost an hour ago.

I'm home from my theater night out with the girls, during which Tabby got a little too tipsy and asked me a

series of embarrassingly intimate questions about Dean
that I refused to answer, and the man himself is still not
home. When someone rings the buzzer, I hurry to answer,
wondering if maybe he lost his key.

But it's not Dean, it's Jack.

Oh boy.

"Lissy," he says when he walks through the door,
unsmiling. "Might want to sit down."

I stare at Jack, wishing a chasm would open up in
the floor and swallow me whole.

"Are you sure?" I repeat.

He's just confirmed everything I'd simultaneously
hoped and feared.

"He had no reason to lie to me," Jack points out.
"And besides, you know how I am at reading people."

"It's a little bit scary," I admit, as my mind races for
any other explanation. One that doesn't involve me being
so wrong. So terribly, terribly wrong.

He's already consoled me, informed me how I
shouldn't beat myself up about it, but what the hell am I
supposed to do now? Things are just too fucked up
between me and Dean. Even if it's really nobody's *fault*, I
can't let go of it.

I'm feeling panicky, like the walls are closing in.
Jack is worried and he wants to make sure I'm okay, but I
need to be alone. I manage to reassure him and shoo him
away, and then I sit down on the bed and I think.

I want M.

I don't care anymore. About the anonymity, the
hostility, or the fact that he's, well, *M*. He's the only thing
in my life that actually makes some kind of twisted sense.

He's right about me. My need for a release, to play at being under somebody's thumb for a while so I don't have to worry about everything.

I don't even care if he's disappointed when he meets me. I have to take that risk. I have to meet the man who makes me feel so...

Alive.

It's a terrible cliché, I admit to myself, as I pack an overnight bag and leave a note for Dean. It just says I'll be back in the morning, and not to tell my family I'm gone. Not that I think he would, but you can't be too careful.

I have no idea how long it'll take M to get to me. I'm afraid to ask. I'm on the verge of losing my nerve already, and when my taxi finally pulls up to the hotel he named, my heart's pounding in my throat.

I get a room for the night, and I can only imagine what the hotel clerk's thinking when I hand over my ID and she sees that I'm local. The elevator ride takes forever, opening the door takes forever, and when I hear the heavy *thunk* behind me as it closes, I wonder what the hell I'm doing.

I can't meet this stranger. Not here. That's not even following basic internet safety rules.

Quickly, I text Jack. I tell him where I am and what I'm doing, and promise to text him a picture of me with the guy so he'll know he can't just murder me and get away with it.

Romantic, Jack comments. I almost laugh, but I can't quite bring myself to manage it.

Then I sit there, and I open up the anonymous messaging app, and I wait.

I try to work up the nerve. My heart is pounding,

my throat dry, and my fingers hover over the buttons. It's so easy. Just three little numbers. He said he'd come. I'm pretty sure he wasn't kidding.

Unless he was, of course. Unless this is some new mindfuck game.

I have to feel out the situation better. Bracing myself for a snarky reply, I type:

I'm at the hotel

He responds almost instantly.

M: That's not a room number, darling.

I know. I need to make sure you're serious about this.

M: When am I ever not?

Constantly. Like all the time. Your job is being sarcastic.

M: Not a job. A hobby. Why are you wasting my time? Either you want to see me, or you don't.

How long would it take you to get here?

M: You won't need to stay more than one night.

That's not what I asked.

M: That's the only answer you get.

I need to know this is real.

Shit. Did I really just type that?

M: That's up to you, isn't it?

He's giving me an out. I have to take it.

I mean, I need to know that you want it to become something else.

Nope. That's way worse.

M: You sound like you're in crisis mode. What's really going on?

You actually want to talk about my problems?

M: Anything's better than talking about our "relationship."

Fair enough, M.

I think I fucked up.

M: You're going to have to be more specific.

With Damien. Obviously.

M: So you run to me. Of course. All right, listen. As a wise man once said, something something, hill of beans, problems of two people, blah blah blah, you'll regret it tomorrow, go back to him.

It's not like that. He's not going to forgive me.

What the hell am I doing? M could turn around and post this on his blog...just like all the sexting we've done...okay, so maybe, for some incomprehensible reason, he's actually taken a liking to me. Or maybe he's setting me up for a spectacular fall.

M: What did you do?

He thinks I don't trust him. And he's right. I don't trust anybody.

M: You trust me.

Oh, fuck. Do I?

I don't trust you. That would be insane.

M: It would be, wouldn't it? And yet, here we are.

Indeed. Here we are.

M: You wouldn't have let any of this happen if you didn't trust me. Trust isn't about never being afraid somebody will fuck you over; it's about deciding to sext them and tell them all the intimate details of your life anyway.

You know if you wrote a motivational book, I would definitely buy it.

M: For you? Free review copy.

I love you.

I've sent it before I can even stop and think about it. It's a joke. *Obviously*, it's a joke. Because you don't fall in love with snarky strangers over the internet, even if you have seen some very flattering pictures of their penis.

It takes a while for him to answer.

M: Of course you do. I'm very lovable.

Thank *fuck*, he gave me an out. Why is my heart pounding so fast?

I guess the problem is that I don't know how to act *like I trust people, then.*

M: Once you've been fucked over enough times, you just have to go with your instincts. Probably they'll be wrong most of the time, especially yours, but what the hell else do we have to go on?

Thanks. Great talk.

M: Think about it. Did you start sexting me because it seemed like a good idea after a lot of careful consideration, or did you do it because I turned you on so much you couldn't help yourself?

Well, that's really not accurate, but I take your point.

M: Someday, Lana, and I truly believe this, someday you'll meet a man in real life who makes you just as miserable and horny as I make you. And it'll feel right. You won't be able to help yourself. You'll have to trust him, because your libido cannot be denied.

Thanks. That's...really sweet, actually.

And then, in the back of my mind, unbidden: *but I already found you.*

I can't possibly explain the connection I've developed with M, or why it feels the way it does. Weirdly *right*, considering how incredibly wrong it is. I have to keep reminding myself that he's a stranger, because he's never really felt like one.

M: I can be surprisingly sweet. Just don't let it slip through your fingers when he comes along. It has to be soon. Third time's the charm, right?

Suddenly, my phone starts ringing. It's Dean. I want to decline the call, but he's probably just going to worry if I don't pick up.

"What the hell's going on, Lissy?" he demands. "You can't just disappear on me like this if we're supposed to be in a relationship. I told your family you've got a dinner meeting, you know they're going to flip out if they know you're out of town."

"I'm not out of town," I tell him. "I was just meeting a friend. I wasn't sure I'd be home tonight, but..."

He's silent for a few minutes. "Okay," he says, finally. I refuse to explain myself any further, daring him to ask. To care. To admit that it's not *just* sex between us. But all I hear on the other end of the phone is calm, steady breathing.

"Dean?" I don't know what I'm about to say, but if I don't say it now, I'm going to lose my nerve.

"I'm here."

"I'm sorry I was a shitty girlfriend."

It comes out before I have a chance to rethink it. I stand up, pace the length of the room, and then sit down again on the end of the bed.

"You weren't a shitty girlfriend," Dean says, quietly. "I'm sorry I lied."

A very long silence stretches between us.

"I know," I tell him, finally. "I just wish..."

"Lissy," he says softly. "Come home."

I do.

CHAPTER THIRTEEN

Third Time's the Charm

I can hardly look at Dean, let alone talk to him. My mood swings wildly from hating him for lying to hating myself for not believing him when he told the truth. How am I supposed to wrap my head around this?

Something's been bothering me, and I can't quite put my finger on it. I feel strange and unbalanced in the back of my mind, like I've been missing something important.

I keep coming back to what M said to me, after his little inspirational speech, and right before Dean called.

Third time's the charm.

That's what he said. Third time's the charm. Because there was Andrew, and then there was Dean, and...

But M doesn't know about any of that. I never told him about Andrew. Granted, over half of our conversations happened while I was drunk, but we didn't start talking about my personal life until Dean moved in.

My throat starts to go dry. I pull up my phone and begin to scroll through the message history, fumbling for a search function or something in this stupid app. But how will I even find it? I wouldn't have mentioned him by name.

You didn't mention him at all, and you know it.

But what does that mean?

I don't know what else to do, so I call Jack.

It rings five times before he picks up.

"This better be good," he warns me. "I just bought drinks for two models from Switzerland. And I'm pretty sure they're twins."

"How can you only be *pretty* sure? Ugh. Never mind. Listen, is there something you need to tell me?"

There's a moment of baffled silence on the other end, then he speaks up again, in the most exasperated tone imaginable. "*Twins*, Lissy."

"Possible twins," I remind him. "Anyway, don't have a twin-threesome. It's weird. I know it's a hot fantasy, but think about what you're really doing."

"They're probably not twins," Jack says. "Are you going to tell me why you're cockblocking me?"

I sigh. "Look, have you been secretly texting me on an anonymous messaging app for the last few months? To mess with me?"

There's another moment of silence, and then he bursts out laughing.

"Ladies, excuse me for a minute," I hear him say,

distantly, as if he's moved his phone away from his mouth. Then, louder: "Okay. *Honey*. What the *fuck* is going on with you right now?"

"I knew it couldn't really be you." I'm chewing on the edge of my fingernail, a nervous habit that only comes out when I'm truly at my wit's end. "So, like, you know how you sometimes meet random people online and decide it might be a good idea to have hot, anonymous sexting with a total stranger?"

"Sure," he says, reasonably.

"Well, I did that. Except it wasn't quite some random stranger. It was this guy. He reviews romance novels. He's totally anonymous, he goes by the name M."

"You're fucking James Bond's boss. Got it. So where does the drama start?"

"Be serious for a second, Jack. He's one of those snark-reviewers. You know. He tears books apart for fun. People love it. And honestly, it's pretty damn funny until you're one of the people he's laying into."

"Wait, wait, wait." Jack's laughing again. "Are you telling me that you're having an online affair with a guy who makes fun of your books? I knew you were a little bit of a masochist, but..." He whistles softly. "My apologies for snapping at you earlier. You do *not* disappoint."

"That's not the reason why!" I insist. "He's really...he really knows how to push my buttons. In a good way."

"Sure," Jack says. It sounds like he's chewing on his straw. "Must just be a *coincidence* that you find him so hot."

Damn it. Jack's onto something, and I hate that. It's usually bad news for my sanity.

"Anyway, that's not the point." I sigh again, more heavily this time.

"Hold on, it gets better?" Jack is grinning, I can tell. "Mind if I put you on speaker?"

"I will reach through this phone and murder you with my bare hands," I warn him.

"Just kidding. It's too loud in here anyway. Go on, go on."

"He said something that makes me think..." I'm biting my lip, really thinking about what I'm about to say. "He mentioned something about me that he *shouldn't know*."

"Okay, okay." The noises of the club start to fade as he presumably steps out onto the sidewalk. "Damn, it's cold out here. All right. So your conspiracy theory is...what? That he's somebody you know in real life? Catfishing you? *Why?*"

"I don't know!" I burst out. "That's why I'm pretty sure I'm losing my mind. But I know I didn't tell him some of this stuff."

"Wait, wait, wait." Jack's probably holding up his hand. "So you're basing all of this on your memories of...I'm just guessing here...some not-quite-sober conversations you had with someone in-between sending him pictures of your thong?"

"Okay, just glossing right past that, I know. I know. But I'm positive. We never really had any personal conversations at all until recently, and I know I'd remember it."

"You *know* you'd remember it?" He sounds skeptical. "Lissy, how many times today did you think you'd lost your phone while you were holding it in your hand?"

"Just once," I mutter. "That's not the point, though. I know I can be a little scatterbrained sometimes, but I know I didn't tell him about Andrew. And he just *knew*."

"Well, that's not possible. Did he mention him by name, or are you reading too much into things, like usual?"

"He said 'third time's a charm.'" I take a deep breath, as Jack wraps his head around this. "In the context of relationships and betrayal. He'd have no reason to say that if he didn't know what happened between me and Andrew - and between me and Dean, for that matter, because I didn't actually tell him Dean had done anything wrong. I just said I fucked up because I couldn't trust him. He had no reason to think..."

"As much as I want to make fun of you for reading too much into everything as usual, that is a pretty weird thing to say." He snaps his fingers. "Unless, of course, *you just told him and forgot about it*."

"No, no, no," I insist, my mind racing with this new realization. "I might've told him about Andrew and forgot, but there is no way I told him about Dean. He doesn't even know Dean exists. He thinks Dean is Damien and he thinks I'm still *with* Damien."

"Oh my God, I can't keep up with this Soap Opera Digest bullshit. Wait. Damien's the guy from the book, right? That you based on Dean."

"I didn't base him on Dean," I insist, starting to wonder how true that is. "But because Mergers & Acquisitions was 'based on a true story,' M and everyone else in the world thinks that I'm still with the guy it's about."

"So M thinks he's sexting a married woman?" Jack whistles. "That doesn't seem like your bag."

"Not married," I correct him. "But yes. I know. Normally, just the fact that he's willing to do it would be enough of a turn-off for me. But I guess...I guess I didn't think about it at the time. And then it just kept happening. I don't know how to say no to him."

"You know this is how those Dateline episodes about 'couples who kill' always start," Jack points out. "This M guy, whoever he is, he's just complicating your life even more than it already is. You have to sever."

"I know that, Jack!" I exclaim. "You think I don't know that? But he's the only thing keeping me sane right now. It's just...it's a release. It's somewhere I can go and be nobody but myself. But it's not even me. That's the beauty of it. I can be whoever I want, and I just...I feel *alive*."

He doesn't say anything for a minute. "You know, you're worrying me. I mean - seriously. How much is this obsession with M affecting your life?"

"Not that much," I lie. "It's just...it's fun. Or at least it was. Now, I don't know what to think. There are only two people in the world who know about Andrew and Dean, and if he's not you, that only leaves one option."

For a while, all I hear is the faint noise of traffic and pedestrians.

"You really think it could be him?" Jack asks, finally.

"I don't know." I'm trying to rub the tension headache out of my forehead, but I know it's not going anywhere. "On the surface, it doesn't seem to make any sense. The timing, for one. Sometimes I got texts from him when Dean was right nearby, or even in the same room. But he must know Dean, right? Or you."

"Right," says Jack. "Because I make a habit of

telling all the mundane details of your life to everyone I know."

"You've never told *anyone*?"

"Why would I?" He lets out a bewildered laugh. "Listen, Lissy - I'm freezing to death. I have to go. But try to think through the rational explanations first. You have to absolutely, categorically eliminate the possibility that you might've told him, or at least given him enough information that he could vaguely reference the situation without really knowing the details. Because, really, there has to be a rational explanation for this. I know you're always looking for conspiracies with that writer brain of yours, but it's *got* to be something simple."

My mind won't stop racing.

It has to be something simple.

That's what Jack said to me. And he was right - nothing in real life is ever as complicated as the stuff I can dream up for my books. It just seems like a hell of a coincidence, unless...

Unless, of course, it wasn't.

Unless, of course, *I* accidentally created M.

Heart pounding, I flip open my computer. I have to double-check the publication date on my first book, The New Haven, to make absolutely sure - because yes, I am that girl who searches for her phone while she's holding it. But that doesn't mean I'm wrong about this.

I cross-check the date with some of the early posts on M's blog. It takes me a second to dig through the archives; he's made them a bit harder to find, it seems like, to the point where I wonder if some of his regular readers would ever think to poke around this deep.

It kind of makes sense. When he started out, he was a much kinder, gentler M. I've looked at some of his older reviews before, and they didn't have any of the bite he developed later. So maybe it was really just a marketing ploy - although clearly, it's become a pretty important part of his personality, even if it wasn't before.

I remember now, when I first started out, I was always picking Dean's brain for his marketing know-how. I explained to him how there were all these book blogs out there, and some of them had a crazy amount of influence, and sometimes I thought he was just pretending to be interested. But maybe I got through, more than I realized.

I start combing through the blog archives. Yes, his first post dates back to just a month or so before I published my first book.

And then, I notice something I've never noticed before.

REVIEW: *The New Haven, by Lana DeVane*

Frowning, I click on it. The beginning of the post is just rehashing the plot of the book, blah blah blah - I scroll down to the end, to get to the good stuff.

FIVE STARS - RECOMMENDED

What?
There are fifty comments on the post, most of them from nearly a year later. I start skimming through them, stomach clenching slightly at the words.

TRACKBACK: Hey, check it out, guys. Looks like M wasn't always so snarky. All his other posts from this time period are books you'd recognize, and then there's this...when a new blogger starts out reviewing an unknown author, you have to wonder what the connection is there... [Read entire post]

Wow. Just wow.

I can't believe you used to be just like the rest of them. Coddling authors and treating them like their books are precious babies. At least you came to your senses, I guess?

So has anyone else seen the theory that M either knows Lana DeVane or is secretly her? Because I read this book and I can't think of any other reason why this review would exist.

People change. I don't know why everyone is piling on M. We don't know the whole story.

Please. It's pretty easy to figure out what's going on here. Be very interested to see if M actually addresses this. I'm not holding my breath.

Seriously? I'm disappointed in you, M...

My heart squeezes with the realizations that are crashing down on me, all at once. M...Dean...might've started this blog with the intention of helping me, not hurting me. He didn't tell me because he knew I'd hate it, wanting my book to sink or swim on its own merits.

After everything fell apart between us, just like magic, M became the king of snark.

The timeline is almost perfect. His review of *Mergers & Acquisitions* showed up shortly after someone discovered his old review of *The New Haven*, judging by the timestamps on the comments. It was the perfect opportunity to regain some credibility that he'd lost by trying to help me. And, I suspect, to work through some of the unresolved hostility between us.

Could it possibly be? Maybe Jack was right in the first place. Maybe I really *am* such a scatterbrain that I told M some of my deepest, darkest secrets and completely forgot. Maybe I'm just grasping at straws, searching for connections that aren't there.

It's hard to imagine Dean being so cold. Then again, what he said to me that night after the fetish ball...

He really thought I hated him.

Yes, he shouldn't have lied. Yes, he could have fought harder to win my trust again. Yes, our relationship was plagued by a thousand little problems that neither one of us wanted to admit, let alone deal with, and he's at least half responsible for that. But the moment I saw him with Jessica, I shut him out. Not because I hated him, because I loved him so much. Because it was too painful.

And in that moment, I hardly cared what the nature of their relationship was. It didn't matter, really. Because no matter what, it meant that I wasn't enough. I couldn't be everything to him.

I did try, once or twice. I offered to take up running so he wouldn't have to be alone. I thought we could motivate each other. But he was always going for too long, or too fast, or he was training for something and it just wasn't a good time to jog along with some slowpoke who was huffing and puffing her way up the sidewalk. He didn't put it exactly in those terms, but he didn't need to.

He rejected me. I told myself I shouldn't care, didn't care, because it was completely understandable. Running was just His Thing. He didn't want me interfering. That was fine.

But it turned out running wasn't just His Thing. It was *Their* Thing.

And that was it, really. By the end of our relationship, there was so little that we shared. I struggled to think of anything we had in common, aside from the fact that we lived together and occasionally had sex.

I don't care if I was cold, that doesn't excuse the things he said about me as M.

Then again -

I think of all the times M actually made an effort to make me feel better, to try and take care of me. I couldn't come up with an explanation for it, but now...

I remember the other thing Jack said.

He's still in love with you.

CHAPTER FOURTEEN

The Park

Dean

"So, you've got the ring?" Bea's eyes glitter as she hovers by me.

"Yes." I'm hoping my gritted teeth pass for a genuine smile.

I don't know what the hell is going on with Lissy. She's hot and cold, and now she's acting like she doesn't even want to see me. There was no good time for this stupid fucking proposal, but this is probably the worst.

"We've got something amazing planned," Tabby assures me, practically quivering with excitement. "Just be ready when we cue you."

How the hell am I going to put a stop to this? I

can't let it happen, but none of these people will take no for an answer.

At least I already had the ring. It was vintage, my grandmother's, one of the few sentimental things I still keep in my life. It's beautiful, and better made than anything nowadays. Lissy's never been big on jewelry, but I feel like she'd probably appreciate it. If only this were real.

It's about to get *very* real, *very* quickly.

Lissy

"Hey, Arthur." I smile at my brother, nudging him a little with my elbow. "So, what's going on?"

He glances at me, sidelong. "Not much," he says, slowly. "I think the girls are planning something."

I shrug. "They're always planning something, aren't they?"

"Yeah." He smiles a little. "I don't think I ever told you congratulations."

"Thanks. Honestly, I've lost track of who's said what."

"That can happen." He glances at me again. "Must be fun - writing romance novels."

"It's a job," I tell him. "But as far as jobs go, yeah...it doesn't get a lot more fun than this."

"I would've figured Mom and Dad would be a little more..." He shrugs. "Judgmental. I don't know."

"Well, they just want us to be happy." I sigh a little as I notice Tabby and Stephanie orbiting around Dean like he's some kind of rockstar. "It's just that, you know...they don't always trust us to know exactly what's right for ourselves. You have to remember, there's a part of them that still pictures us crawling around in diapers and trying to eat dirt off the floor. It's a hard adjustment to make."

"Yeah." Arthur's staring at his shoes.

"Come on, there's something going on with you," I say, as jovially as I can manage. "What is it? Your secret's safe with me."

He shrugs uncomfortably. "It's nothing."

"It's obviously not nothing." I smile at him. "But if you really, really don't want to tell me - that's fine. Just know it's an option. Okay?"

Arthur is silent for a few minutes.

"I kind of hate my job," he says, finally.

My parents, bless them, have been pushing him into auto body repair since he was about three years old. He showed a vague interest in cars once, as most kids do - it's a symbol of the freedom you crave so badly before you realize that being responsible for your own life actually sucks.

"Well, have you..."

"Botany," he says before I can finish my sentence. "I just...I like plants, you know? There's so much about them that we still don't understand."

"Really?" That one's new by me. "Uh...well, you know, that's...you should definitely do it. I'm not sure exactly what botanists do in the work force, but..."

"Museums, natural parks, consulting companies, the federal government...there's a jillion career opportunities," he assures me, his eyes lighting up. "I already looked into programs, and...and..."

"So, what's stopping you?" I already know the answer.

He sighs, looking down at the ground again. "Can you imagine Dad's face?"

I can.

"Look, Arthur...they don't really get me, either. They never have. But Mom and Dad really do love us, that much I know. They might be confused at first, or even upset, but at the end of the day...they just want to see us smile. They want to see us achieve whatever will make us feel fulfilled."

I wasn't even aware of how true it was until I said it. Clapping Arthur on the shoulder, I take a look at our surroundings for the first time in a while. We've been walking for several blocks to an unknown destination, and I've just been following my dad's hideous yellow tourist shirt like a homing beacon. I wasn't really paying attention, until...

We're right across from the park.

The park where I saw Dean and Jessica jogging together.

I take a deep breath, reminding myself, somewhat forcefully, and everything's going to be okay. Sure, I've avoided this park, this block, this entire area for the last few years. I didn't know how I'd react. It's been a long time, and now I know the truth.

Of course, that doesn't make it any easier.

I remember, in vivid detail, exactly how it felt to be sitting there and witnessing something so devastating. But now, with the added bonus of knowing just how much I misunderstood it...

We're crossing towards the park. Dean glances back at me with a look on his face that mirrors almost exactly what I'm feeling, except there's something else.

Something he knows that I don't know.

"Come on, this looks like the perfect spot for a family portrait!" My mom is beckoning us all towards the lake, and I walk like I'm being propelled there, just putting one foot in front of the other, wishing I could keep walking until I was in the water, letting it go up past my head.

My family all clusters in an awkward group, like they've never taken a damn portrait before. Nothing could be further from the truth, so what the hell is going on, exactly?

I'm concentrating very hard on breathing, slow and steady, so I almost don't notice the elaborate series of hand gestures and stage whispers my mom is directing towards Dean.

Oh, no.

Oh, God no.

In the split second it takes for him to approach me, a lifetime passes. I remember all the time my mother cooed and gasped over public proposals, especially the ones that included family.

She's orchestrated this.

She's gone behind my back and...

My breathing is no longer in control. I'm hyperventilating. There's an unspoken apology in Dean's face as he goes down on one knee, holding up a little velvet box towards me.

I can see his lips moving, but I can't even begin to comprehend the words that are coming out of his mouth. My throat is closing up and I can't do this. I can't.

But then I realize everyone in my family is staring at me expectantly, and I force my head to jerk forward. Once.

A nod.

That's enough to make them erupt into cheers, along with a few jovial bystanders. Dean slips the ring onto my finger and it fits perfectly, of course, because he was in on it too.

I'm pretty sure I'm gasping like a beached fish, and I must look like death, because my mom rushes over to me with a sudden frown on her face.

"Honey, are you okay?"

It doesn't take her long to recognize that my face is not streaked with tears of happiness. Mother's intuition, indeed. She wraps me into a hug to conceal her urgent whispers.

"Honey, I'm so sorry. I thought...I thought you would love this. What's wrong?"

"N...nothing," I manage to choke out, fooling absolutely no one. "Nothing, Mom."

My whole family is uncomfortably silent. I turn to Dean.

"Can I talk to you for a second?" I rasp out.

He nods, leading me around a little copse of trees while my family shuffles their feet anxiously.

"I'm so sorry," he whispers, as soon as we're out of earshot. "I knew about the proposal, obviously, but I had no idea they would be bringing us *here*."

"You knew?" I echo. He obviously did, but I still can't wrap my head around it.

"Your parents have been..." He grimaces. "Your mom, at least, she's been planning this for a while. She sort of..."

I don't want to hear it. "And you didn't *tell* me?"

I'm aware my voice is becoming shrill, but I can't

control it. I feel like I'm losing my grip on reality. My heart and head are pounding, and all I want to do is tell him *I KNOW. I KNOW WHO YOU REALLY ARE.*

But I don't.

"I have to get out of here," I tell him, my voice shaking. "Just...figure something out. Make an excuse. I have a migraine. We were fighting earlier. Whatever. I just need..."

"I understand," Dean says, softly. "I'll take care of it."

Of course he will. He's the goddamn king of everything.

I'm running.

I'm halfway to the hotel that M told me about, before I even realize where I'm going.

Because I need the answer. I need to know. I need to check in, while the clerk tries not to look like she's staring, with my hair tangled and wild. I need to snatch the key and go into my room and take one moment, just one moment, to reconsider while the door clicks shut behind me.

So I do.

Then I open the app on my phone.

I tap on M's name.

Then, I text him three little numbers.

CHAPTER FIFTEEN

Meeting M

I pull the door open, and I look at him. Calmly. My heart is about to beat out of my chest, but I just look at him like he's coming to deliver my morning paper.

Of course it's Dean. Of course.

Occam's Razor. The simplest explanation is always the best.

It doesn't take more than a split second for him to realize that I'm not shocked.

"Just curious," I say, still standing in the half-open doorway. "What were you planning on telling me when you walked in here?"

"Honestly?" His hands are shoved deep in his pockets, ruining the line of his suit. "I was just going to wing it. It's worked pretty well for me so far."

"You have a lot of explaining to do," I inform him.

"I'm aware," he says. "Are you going to make me do it in the hallway?"

I step aside to let him in. He paces the room for a second, pausing at the window, staring out at the city lights like they're going to help him get through this, somehow.

"You're smart," he says. "Smart enough to send your friend after me to find out if I was a liar. I'm sure you've pieced it together already, for the most part."

Damn it, Jack. "Was it that obvious?"

He shrugs. "Not at first. Everything I told him was true. But he's pretty damn good at getting people to talk. He should probably think about hosting Taxicab Confessions."

"I've always said that." Maybe I should feel mortified. I don't know. Although I'd started to suspect, I needed to hear the truth from someone I could trust.

"I figured out that you probably created M to help me," I admit. "Which is...sweet, if misguided."

He nods, still facing away from me. "I knew you'd hate it. You and your integrity. So I figured, it couldn't hurt you if you just...never knew about it. Anyway, I wanted to do it. Once you told me about the online book world, I got kind of fascinated. From a marketing perspective, it's a whole different ecosystem with its own rules and exploits. I justified it as market research. I mean, let's be honest, are big ad agencies like mine going to be around forever?"

He shrugs, mostly to himself. "Of course not. Things are changing all the time now, and faster every day. These days, with communication so fast and easy compared to what it used to be, grassroots marketing is the next big thing. I wanted to play around in that sandbox."

"Those are real people, you know," I point out. "Real people who really trusted your opinion, and you were just using them as guinea pigs?"

"At first," he admits. "But then I really started to enjoy it. People actually *wanted* and *valued* my opinions. It was the complete opposite of my job. Nobody told me that my copy wasn't good enough, or that I needed to 'make it pop,' or that it didn't 'feel right' and I should scrap the idea they already approved last month and start over. Not once. It was just pure, unadulterated appreciation. Maybe I let it go to my head, a little bit."

"Maybe," I snort.

"I really do feel bad about that Mergers & Acquisitions review," he says, finally turning to look at me. "At the time, it seemed like the only way to get my credibility back."

"And piss me off," I point out.

He shrugs. "That wasn't a primary goal."

"Please."

"Fine. Maybe I was feeling a little vindictive." He paces the length of the room again. "But I knew you were a tough cookie. You could take it. There's no such thing as bad publicity, anyway. If I really thought it would hurt you, I never would've published it. But everything I criticized about the book is shit that plenty of people love. That's just how it works."

He pauses, sort of half-smiling a little. "For the record, I actually liked the book a lot."

"Wow." I sit down on the end of the bed, crossing my legs. "Your vote of confidence is overwhelming."

Dean sighs, pulling out the desk chair and sitting

down. "Here's the thing, Lissy, I never meant for any of this to go down the way it did. After the review came out, I kept waiting for some kind of reaction from you. I don't know what I expected, but I thought...I don't know. It started to bug me that you were acting like it just didn't exist. And that's where I should've just let it go. It was petty of me."

I have to laugh a little bit. "Right. That was petty. The review itself, on the older hand...totally justified."

"I didn't say it was," he cuts in, shaking his head. "Even if I really did hate it, I would've felt bad about saying so. But the fact that I lied, just to boost my own credibility - well, I do have a conscience. I shouldn't have used you like that. Even knowing you'd be okay, it was wrong. I should've just let it go. My whole 'scandal' would have blown over anyway, but I didn't give it a chance. I thought I needed to do damage control." He sighs. "And then, I started poking at you. I guess I just wanted an excuse to reconnect. It was so hard to understand what you were thinking after the shit went down...I realized I had this opportunity to get to know you, all over again. Of course that's not how I expected it to go, not at first. At first I figured you'd tell me to go fuck myself if I tried to talk to you."

A wry smile tugs at my mouth. "Didn't realize how much of a masochist I really am."

"Guess I didn't," he admits, with an answering half-grin. "That's what I get for underestimating you once again."

"So the sexting thing..."

"It wasn't calculated," he says. "I swear. I never intended for things to go in that direction, because, well, it was a bad idea. You caught me at a weird time. I was drunk and horny and I figured, hey, why the hell not. I can fool around with her, she'll never find out it was me, it's harmless, it'll be fun. I never intended to do a repeat performance. Certainly not...*dozens*."

My voice is soft and demure. I hardly recognize it. "It *was* pretty addictive, wasn't it?"

"Very," he says, still smiling. "After you called and asked me to help out with your little 'based on a true story' problem, well, I figured I'd just quit. There was no way I could maintain the two identities while we were living together. But I found a way. That app has a handy little scheduling feature, for one."

Oh, for fuck's sake.

"Of course." I'm laughing at myself. "God bless technology."

There's a hint of nostalgia in Dean's eyes. "I have to admit it was fascinating, getting to know that side of you. I'd never seen it before. Not even close. You were so passionate, and wild, and for a while I was just angry that you'd never bothered to show *me* any of that. Then I started wondering if maybe I didn't deserve it, because I didn't try. M gave me a chance to start over. To really give you the kind of man you'd always wanted in your life."

I hug my knees against my chest. "You thought I was cold."

"I did." He nods. "I thought you'd just...I don't know, Lissy. I thought all kinds of things, to try and explain how things broke down between us. It took me a long time to really accept how much of it was my fault. I wanted you to trust me, but I didn't want to do the work to earn it. And at the same time, from the beginning, I knew I didn't really deserve it. Not when I was lying to you all along. I wanted you, but I wanted some version of you that had never been hurt before. But that's unfair. I realize that now. Everybody comes with baggage."

"Even you?" I raise an eyebrow at him.

"Even me," he admits. "This might shock you, but I'm *not* perfect."

"Wow, you've really grown as a person."

He pinches the bridge of his nose, briefly, as he shuts his eyes. "God. I haven't even gotten to the proposal yet. Look, your parents..."

"It's okay," I reassure him. "I know how they can be. I mean...it's not okay, but I know it's not entirely your fault."

"They really did come in like a hurricane," he admits. "Your mother insisted that you wanted a public proposal in front of the whole family, and if I hadn't picked up on that, it was just because I lacked *a mother's intuition*." He grimaces. "I knew you'd be pissed off that I talked to them alone, so I figured I'd just humor her, and keep putting it off. But that's not really possible, with your clan."

"No, it is not." I smile, sympathetically. "That absolutely sucked, but at least it got us here."

"Is this really what you wanted?" Dean leans forward, locking his eyes with mine. I want to look away, because it's too much, with all of these revelations coming so quickly and stacking on top of each other to the point where I'm not sure who I'm looking at anymore. But I don't. "Wouldn't you rather M just stay safe and untouched in the lockbox of your imagination? He could be anybody. He could be a secret agent. Instead of..."

He drifts off, like he's searching for some kind of

epithet to describe himself, and comes up short. What is he to me, these days? What do I *want* him to be?

"No," I tell him softly. "I'm glad it's you. I wouldn't rather it be anybody else."

And it's true, to my surprise. Dean's eyes soften a little.

"I'm sorry I could never be what you needed before," he says, his voice a little lower and quieter. "I'm sorry I took you for granted."

"I'm sorry I didn't tell you what I wanted," I admit, feeling my cheeks grow hot. "I just...I didn't know how."

"I know," he says. His tongue briefly flicks out to lick his lips. "I don't blame you."

"I figured you wouldn't want to," I confess. "I figured there was no point, because you'd just laugh it off or call me weird or...I don't know. Something."

"I wouldn't have," he says. "But I don't think I was ready, either. You can't be a Dom and be selfish. I thought it was the opposite, at first, but it's all about caring for somebody. Trying to anticipate their needs, and know them better than they know themselves. That's what all relationships should be, really. And I never put in that kind of energy for you. I never put in the effort."

Something has changed in the air between us. A tension sparked, thickening, and I know this isn't the right time to let things go in that direction, but right now? I don't care.

I stare at Dean, and he stares back.

"I can't stop thinking about spanking you," he confesses, his eyes burning into mine. "I'm going to hell, right?"

"At least you won't be alone there." I lick my lips,

standing up slowly. His gaze never leaves me as I slip out of my jeans and clamber onto the bed, on my hands and knees.

"No," he says, softly, beckoning me towards him with one finger.

Well, all right then.

I come towards him and I pause, standing next to him, staring down at his lean, powerful thighs, where I'm supposed to drape my body. I'm biting my lip.

"If you want it, this is how it's going to be," he says, quietly. Firmly.

I do it. My feet still dangle on the floor, and I'm grabbing the edge of the desk to support myself, to keep all the blood from rushing to my head. Not that there will be much danger of that, once he starts.

"I know it seems strange," he says, his hand resting on my ass. "But this is my apology. It's also your atonement. But I think it can be both, and I think, for us at least, that actually makes some kind of twisted sense."

I nod.

The first smack is gentle. Loving. It wasn't what I expected, but then again, nothing that's happened between us is necessarily what you'd expect.

"It took me a long time to really understand," he says, softly, before the next one lands. A little harder, but still not enough to make me jump. "The reason I was so angry, the reason it was easy to almost...almost hate you, for a while, after it happened...was because of how much I loved you."

Smack.

"It seems obvious now. But I didn't get it at the time. And then, with M...I thought it was just fun to mess with you. I'll be honest. I liked that I could make you vulnerable, because I felt like you'd shut me out. I felt like you'd always been shutting me out, since the beginning."

Smack. It's harder this time. I squirm, feeling him stiffen underneath me.

"Pretty soon, though, it was more than that. I think you felt it too. Fuck that, I *know* you did. Am I right?"

I swallow, hard. "Yes."

Smack.

"I didn't want to accept it, especially after we started playing house. It was too dangerous. It was such a bad idea, with so many pitfalls, and so many reasons to walk away. I was going to kill off M, and after the 'relationship' was over I'd shake your hand, and I'd never see you again. That was the plan." There's a sharp intake of breath as his hand drifts down between my legs, feeling me grow hot and wet for him. "But then you kissed me."

Smack.

I laugh, a little breathlessly. "Is that for the kiss?"

"Yes. And no." His other hand strokes my hair, and I let out a little noise that's almost a purr. "Because it also made me realize something I don't think I would have let myself, otherwise."

I don't realize I'm holding my breath until he speaks again.

"I still love you, Lissy."

I fill my lungs with one sharp gasp.

"I'm not saying that so you'll say it back," he murmurs.

Smack.

"I'm saying it," he goes on, "because you deserve to know. This isn't just about punishments and corsets and unresolved tension from years ago. This isn't about me wanting a second chance to prove myself to you. That's all part of it, but that was all just leading to the inevitable conclusion."

Smack.

"I love you. I loved you when I first saw you, and I was scared to lose you, and that's why I lied. I didn't know how to love you back then. It was all a mess and it was mostly my fault for not knowing you, and not *trying* to know you. It seemed so complicated and difficult when it was really very simple."

Smack.

I'm panting now, excitement heavy in my belly, but I'm fighting to focus on his words.

He still loves me.

"I was afraid to know you," he says, at last. "I was afraid to find out that you were beyond me. I was afraid to find out that I couldn't be what you needed, so I just let things stay the way they were. I never asked the questions I didn't want to know the answers to."

Smack.

"And you deserved more than that. Better than that. No, Lissy, you weren't blameless, but I'm the one who set the tone. How could I expect you to trust me, when I didn't trust *you*?"

And that's it.

That's the one thing I've never quite been able to put my finger on, the fatal flaw in our relationship. And he's managed to put words to it, before I even could.

"Dean," I moan, and I feel him hesitate, his hand ready to strike. "Dean, I l..."

"Stop," he commands. "Not now. You're

emotionally compromised. You're drunk on hormones. If you still feel it afterwards, tell me then."

Smack.

This one is hard, but that's not what makes the tears spring to my eyes. He's right. But I know this goes deeper. I never stopped loving him either, and without knowing it, that's why I was so desperate to connect with M. I felt the same bond with him, and now I understand why.

His fingers dip low again, and I gasp.

"Please," I whisper. "I need..."

"What?" he whispers back, his hand stilling.

"I want to make love," I confess.

Yes, that's right. I want to make love to the man who called me frigid and frustrated. I want to make love to the liar, the dominant, the man who wore leather pants just because I asked him to.

For once, I don't want to fuck. I want more.

He's lifting me up now, so he can stand and lead me to the bed. I stretch out underneath him, luxuriating in the desire that radiates from him.

A moment later he's close to me, so close that our foreheads almost touch. I need him closer.

"Are you sure?" he asks, his voice heavy with lust.

I'm nodding before I even understand the question. He's asking because we haven't done it like this, not face-to-face, since we were still a couple.

Yes, I'm sure.

A moment later, he pushes inside me with a soft groan. I watch how his face changes, drinking it in, seeing everything I've missed, all the things I've never seen before.

I wrap my legs around him, and I lose myself in the feeling. It's slow and steady at first, then faster, harder, faster, and I'm pretty sure the headboard is shaking and I'm not sure if this counts as lovemaking anymore.

And I really, really don't care.

I realize that I'm begging for more, panting his name, gripping the wooden slats behind my head and trying to keep from moaning too loud. The bed is creaking in time with every sharp thrust, and I -

"*Ah*," I cry out, because that's as quiet as I can possibly be when he pushes me over the edge.

Moments later, he follows, panting and shuddering in my arms. It's a rare moment of weakness for a man who dominated my life and my heart in two separate identities.

It's worth treasuring, even though I know there will be many more.

A few moments later, he rolls off of me and pulls me close again, pillowing my head against his chest. The sound of his heartbeat brings me back down to earth. Slowly.

I don't know how long we've been lying there, but the floaty sensation is starting to go away. I feel grounded, my euphoria slowly being replaced by contentment.

"Dean, I..."

"Look at me," he interrupts, stroking the side of my cheek with his thumb. I do.

His eyes are calm and clear, and I hope mine are, too. I know why he's doing this. He has to make sure it's real.

"Yes, Lissy?" His breath is warm brushing past my face. He's almost smiling, but not quite.

"I love you." The words come out so easily, despite

the weight of them. I'm almost shocked at how easily. Like the feeling never left, because of course it didn't.

His smile finally comes to life, breaking like sunshine across his face.

"I loved you when you were a snarky bastard who wanted to see my panties," I tell him. "I loved you when you told me that someday I'd learn to trust somebody again. And when you told me I should wear a bikini."

I take a deep breath, and go on.

"I loved you the day I saw you with her. I loved you when you came home. I loved you when you left."

My eyes are swimming in tears, and I'm not even sure when it happened.

"It never stopped, not even when I wanted it to. I loved you when I hated you, and once I realized you'd never really cheated, that you only lied because you didn't want to lose your friend...I was devastated."

"I know," he says, softly. Finally. That smile just won't go away. "That was me you came and cried to, remember?"

"Right." My cheeks are turning red. "Of *course* I remember."

"It's a little bit hard to keep track," he says. "Hence, my fatal mistake."

"Third time's the charm." I grin. "You know, it took me a while to notice."

"I thought you might not notice at all," he admits. "But I panicked right after I sent it. That's why I called you. I was hoping it would be enough of a distraction."

"It almost was," I tell him. "But I knew something wasn't right. Jack said I must've told you...meaning M...at some point, and forgotten about it. But I was sure I hadn't.

That didn't make any sense. The only thing that made any sense was..."

"I'm just glad you get it now," he says, and I'm pretty sure I know what he's referring to.

"I do," I reply. "And I'm so...so sorry that things happened the way they did. Jessica..."

He smiles, a little wistfully. "*That* was almost entirely my fault. It looked just as suspicious to her as it did to you. She thought I was secretly in love with her, because otherwise why would I lie? That was really what drove her away, not the fact that you and I were breaking up."

"It's shitty anyway." I let my eyes drift away from his, down past his neck, to his chest, all the solid planes of muscle intersecting. "I love Jack to death. I'd be wrecked if something like that happened. But I was just...when everything went down, I was so angry, I couldn't possibly see things from your point of view. I was just trying to protect myself."

"I know," he says. "Fool me twice, shame on me."

"Exactly. It felt like...if I let you pull the wool over my eyes, it would be my fault, more than yours." I suck in a deep breath. "Because I should know better."

He shakes his head a little. "It always used to drive me crazy, you know - the way you beat yourself up. You're smart as hell, Lissy. Everybody makes mistakes. Everybody's a little bit stupid sometimes."

I giggle, softly.

"What?" he demands, smiling a little.

"You sound like *him*."

"He sounds like me," Dean corrects me. "I came first."

"Right, of course." I'm still laughing. "I just can't believe I didn't piece it together until now."

"I can't imagine why you would have," Dean says. "If I hadn't gotten my storylines mixed up..."

"But he always sounded just like you," I point out.

He smiles, stroking my hair back from my face. "Lissy, listen. I didn't understand why you shut me out. I do now. I took you for granted, and I promise I won't let that happen again." He pauses, just breathing for a minute. "Do you promise the same for me?"

"Yes," I whisper, without having to think about it. "Yes."

And for now, that's good enough.

CHAPTER SIXTEEN

Wanted

In the end, everybody got what they wanted.

I got to be with the man I'd fallen for, over a series of dirty text messages, because he was the same man I'd loved all along. Dean got a chance to prove himself as a changed man, he best lover and the best dominant anyone could possibly ask for. We're even going to see the new Paranormal Activity together. I promised him that if the movie turns out to be tedious, we'll find a way to make it interesting.

Jack got to sleep with those twins, but he did admit that I was right - it was a weirder experience than he was expecting. We don't hang out quite as much now, but he's still my go-to for any life drama that would make Dean roll his eyes too far. He and Dean have a cordial understanding. They are friendly, but not *too* friendly, because the last thing I need is a conflict of interest between my fiancé and my best friend. Jack is my confidant, and occasionally, that requires him to side against Dean. That's just the way it goes.

Oh, right. The ring. I guess I got ahead of myself there. I never did end up taking it off, because I was afraid I'd forget to put it back on again when I saw my family. Eventually, I just leave it there, because it feels right.

The actual proposal happens very quietly and without fanfare, as we slip into bed together one evening in the spring.

"So, do you...do you actually want to get married?"

Dean has that look on his face like he's ready to play it off as a joke at a moment's notice, if necessary.

I glance down at my hand. "Well, did you mean it when you asked me?"

"I kind of did," he confesses. "It's all I've really wanted for a long time."

"Really?"

He nods, sliding his arms around me. "I already lost you once. I'm not letting you slip through my fingers again."

So even my parents got what they wanted - a big, public spectacle of a proposal, even if it's not quite what anyone thought it would be. Tabby helps me with venues, Stephanie is dealing with all the decorating, and Nick is finding the band while Scott does the first round of eliminations for the bakeries. Arthur wants to handle the flowers, and I'm very proud of the fact that nobody in my family feels the need to make fun of him for it. Even Dean takes more of an active interest than I would have expected. He's still capable of surprising me.

"What do you think of getting married in an art museum?" I hand Dean the pamphlet across the breakfast table on a lazy Saturday morning.

"Sounds expensive," he says, smiling. "Won't your dad be upset that it's not a church?"

"He'll get over it." I shrug. "He only *acts* super-traditional because he feels like it's his only identifying personality trait now that he's getting older. I'm just grateful he skipped over the typical midlife crisis, sports car, younger woman thing."

"Small mercies," Dean agrees. "It does look nice, but are they one of those places that charge an extra fee for cake-cutting or any of that 'we're happy to bleed brides dry because we think they're irrational' bullshit?"

I chuckle. "I'll make sure and ask when I call. What difference does it make? It's a wedding, everything's overpriced."

"It's the principle of the thing," he mutters. "Shouldn't you be getting all riled up about this? They only do it because weddings are traditionally planned by women. Girl power, and all that?"

Laughing, I reach for his hand and clasp it between my fingers. He sighs, relaxing a little. "Honestly? This is the least girl-power sentiment you'll ever hear from me, but after everything that's happened, I'm just glad I'm finally marrying you."

His eyes lock with mine, and his smile is nothing but genuine love. "Don't screw it up."

"Right back at you." I glance back down at the massive notebook in front of me. "Do you think we should invite the Risingers? Meg said they wanted to come when we were hanging out at that convention in Florida, but I think that might've been the whiskey talking."

"Can't hurt," he says. "It's probably not their usual caliber of event, but you know, we can spring for a few ice sculptures if you want."

I make a face. "Is it really bad that I kind of want one? I know it's probably the most ridiculous thing you could possibly spend money on, but..." I sigh, dreamily. "*A swan made out of ice.*"

Dean stands up, coming around to my side of the table and grabbing both my hands in his. When he pulls me to my feet, just for a moment, he actually takes my breath away.

Okay, so maybe I let it happen. But nobody said you couldn't meet a perfect love story halfway.

"You can have all the ice sculptures you want, Lana DeVane," he says, as our noses bump together. "You've earned it."

More from Melanie

Thanks for reading! If you enjoyed this book, please leave a review to let me know - it'll help me figure out what to write next.

Curious about Meg and Adrian's story? Get your copy today by typing this into your browser:

bit.ly/HisSecretary

HIS SECRETARY: UNDONE

I'm about to throw an ashtray at my boss's head.

Turns out, the mind behind my favorite, steamy romance novels...the ones I only read in private...the ones that are my only escape after a long day of dealing with The Boss From Hell? It's not Natalie McBride, the sweet, rural housewife.

It's him.

That's right: my boss, Adrian Risinger, the thirty-three-year-old, maddeningly sexy, pissant billionaire "bad boy" who thinks he runs my life. He is also the author of all my deepest, most secret fantasies. And to make matters worse, he needs me to impersonate "Natalie" at a series of book signings and conventions. But, of course, that's only if I want to keep my job.

On second thought, I'm going to need something heavier than an ashtray.

Read it now! **bit.ly/HisSecretary**

For exclusive content, sales, and special opportunities for fans only, plus a FREE ebook copy of the full-length standalone novel ROMANCE IMPOSSIBLE, please sign up for Melanie's mailing list: **bit.ly/MailingListMel**

You'll never be spammed, and your information will never be shared or sold.

You can also friend her on Facebook: **bit.ly/MelanieFacebook** and like her page: **bit.ly/MelanieFBPage** At her website **melaniemarchande.com** you will find series reading orders, playlists, and contact information for rights inquiries.

CPSIA information can be obtained at www.ICGtesting.com
Printed in the USA
LVOW11s1858190515

439074LV00003B/146/P